# THE PECOS KID

*Other Five Star Titles*
*by Dan Cushman:*


In Alaska with Shipwreck Kelly
Valley of a Thousand Smokes
Blood on the Saddle

# THE PECOS KID

A Western Duo

# DAN CUSHMAN

**Five Star**
Unity, Maine

Five Star Western.
Published in conjunction with
Golden West Literary Agency.

Cover photograph by Robert Darby.

September 1999

Standard Print Hardcover Edition.

First Edition, Second Printing

Five Star Standard Print Western Series.

The text of this edition is unabridged.

Set in 11pt. Plantin by Al Chase.

Printed in the United States on permanent paper.

**Library of Congress Cataloging-in-Publication Data**
Cushman, Dan.
    [Riders of the Gunsmoke Rim]
    The Pecos Kid : a western duo / by Dan Cushman.
— 1st ed.
      p.    cm.
    Contents: Riders of the Gunsmoke Rim —
The Deadwood drive.
    ISBN 0-7862-1895-9 (hc : alk. paper)
    1. Frontier and pioneer life — West (U.S.) — Fiction.
2. Western stories.  I. Cushman, Dan.  Deadwood drive.
II. Title.  III. Title: Deadwood drive.
PS3553.U738P43  1999
  813'.54—dc21
                                          99-35656

# TABLE OF CONTENTS

# Editor's Note

In the literary history of Western fiction magazines, some of the most popular authors of Western stories have had magazines named after them. *Zane Grey's Western Magazine*, published by Dell Publishing Company, began publication with the November, 1946 issue and continued for eighty-two issues, concluding publication with the issue dated January, 1954. *Max Brand's Western Magazine* was launched by Popular Publications, Inc., with the issue dated December, 1949, and continued for thirty-three issues, concluding with the issue dated August, 1954. *Walt Coburn's Western Magazine* commenced publication from Popular Publications, Inc., with the issue dated November, 1949, and after sixteen issues ceased publication with the issue dated May, 1951. *Louis L'Amour's Western Magazine*, published by Dell Magazines, began with an undated issue published in March, 1994, and continued for twelve issues, concluding with the issue dated January, 1996. *The Pecos Kid Western*, initiated by Popular Publications, Inc., with the first issue dated July, 1950, was a little different. Like *The Masked Rider Western* or *The Rio Kid Western*, pulp magazines published by the competing Standard Magazines, *The Pecos Kid Western* featured a long short novel in every issue about the Pecos Kid, but unlike most of the Western hero pulp magazines all of these stories were written by a single author, Dan Cushman, who had created the character especially for *The Pecos Kid Western*. The year 1950 was not an auspicious time to be creating a new pulp magazine, since pulp magazines were being replaced on newsstands by paperback books, many of them being published by magazine publishers like Dell Publishing. Despite the hostile market in 1950, *The Pecos Kid Western* did continue publication for five issues, concluding with the issue dated June, 1951. The stories about the Pecos Kid that Dan Cushman wrote for this magazine have not otherwise been available since their first publication. The present volume contains the first two short novels Dan Cushman published about the adventures of this fascinating character of the Old West. The remaining short novels will follow in subsequent Five Star Westerns.

# RIDERS OF THE GUNSMOKE RIM

# I

# "ACTION AT NIGHT"

He rode at a steady pace, slowly outdistancing his two companions and the four hundred head of Wyoming stocker cattle they were driving, and finally reined in on a rise of prairie overlooking the limitless badlands and mirage of the Yellowstone country. He had the slouched and easy manner of one who spent as much time in the saddle as out of it. He seemed perfectly relaxed. His eyes had a slow thoughtfulness as they roved and picked out the tiny details of that vast, brown prairie.

He'd been there long enough to smoke his way slowly through a hand-rolled cigarette when his two companions quit their places by the herd and rode up, one on each side of him.

"So, *Señor* Keed," the smaller of the two said, with a handsome flash of teeth from his deeply browned face, "the Yellowstone. The end of the trail . . . no?"

"Sure, Butch, that's the Yellowstone." Then the Kid twisted the left side of his mouth and added: "The hell with it."

William Calhoun Warren, the Pecos Kid, had no particular reason for this condemnation. It was merely a statement of attitude, general in scope, including many things besides the muddy Yellowstone. It was thus his companions accepted it.

"Yes, *señor*. *Sí*. The hell weeth it. To hell with thees hot country . . . the sun, the heat, the dust in the throat. Tonight the Two Bar and more of thees miserable salt pork and beans. But *tomorrow!* Tomorrow the bright light, the sparkle of wine, the laughing *señorita*. So?"

"So. So you get in any more jams and you'll shoot your way out of them by yourself."

The Pecos Kid could remember saying substantially the same thing to Hernandez Pedro Gonzales y Fuente Jesús María Flanagan in McCaffeyville, Arkansas City, and Abilene, in Baker Town, Cheyenne, and in a number of lesser places along the route without once exactly backing up his threat when the chips were down.

"And that goes for you, too, Jimmy, my boy," he said to Big Jim Swing, a huge cowboy with pale eyes and a mass of burlap-colored hair only partly hidden by his California sombrero. "When we get to Miles, you can visit the fleshpots on your own. Oh, the hell with it. Why should I worry about an Irish-Spanish half-breed and two hundred pounds of California saddle tramp?"

"And to hell weeth you, too, *señor!*" Hernandez Flanagan said.

Bill Warren, the Pecos Kid, slouched around in the saddle. His eyes had come to rest on a rattlesnake that had just slid partly from view in a clump of sagebrush. His right hand came up in a movement that was apparently casual, and yet it was weighted with a .44 caliber Colt. It exploded, and he shouted: "Heads!"

The snake writhed into view. Hernandez Flanagan drew an instant later, hesitated half a second, aiming across the saddle horn, and pulled the trigger.

"Tails!"

His slug, traveling with a fine degree of accuracy, had severed the snake's rattles.

Big Jim Swing bent over and picked them up. "Eight," he said.

Hernandez sadly drew a black leather notebook from a saddlebag, wet a stub pencil, and carefully inscribed a figure.

"Thees makes fifty thousand dollars I owe you for snakes alone, *señor*."

"I'll settle for a dollar six bits."

"Ha! Would I be insulted by taking a reduction? Have I not told you? A debt of the Flanagans is never forgotten. Thees moneys will I go on owing you until the last day of time."

Bill Warren laughed. It relaxed the lean, dehydrated lines of his face and gave it a fleeting, boyish expression. A person seeing him at that moment would have found it hard to believe he was the man whose guns had burned the reputation of the Pecos Kid from the Río Grande to Montana. He loaded up and said: "You boys go back and keep those cows drifting toward water. Springs yonder. I'll ride down to the Two Bar."

The Pecos Kid touched his blunt, star-roweled spurs and let his sorrel cayuse take an easy pace down descending benches toward the scattered buildings and corrals of the Two Bar. A slight breeze was coming from the badlands of the Yellowstone, so he slid back his Confederate cavalry hat to get the feel of it in his unruly red hair.

He noticed there were no horses in the corrals. No one around. His instincts, long trained in the anticipation of trouble, caused him to ease back on the bridle and take the last two hundred yards at a slow walk. He noticed a window of stretched antelope skin punched by three round holes near the bottom. Here and there, fresh scars cut through the gray, weathered surface of cottonwood logs. The house had taken a bullet beating, and not long before.

He reined in, shouted: "Hey, in there!"

His voice had a flat sound in the late afternoon heat. He swung down, walked with a tinkle of spurs across the hard-beaten ground, paused at the door. His eyes, long used to sun, were blind for a while—then he made out the main room of the house.

It was a combined kitchen and living room with even a couple of bunks against one wall. A can of flapjack batter stood on the table. A bullet had smashed through near the bottom and most of its contents had run across the table and through its broad cracks. The batter was dry and wrinkled across the surface, but still sticky beneath. It had happened that morning, or the night before.

He walked to the next room. Even darker, there. He kicked an empty cartridge case that jingled across the floor. Empty cases lay everywhere. Forty-Fours, for either a Colt or a Winchester. The room seemed hot and suffocating. Actually it was cooler than outside, but the Pecos Kid, like many who spent most of their time outdoors, had an aversion and suspicion of houses.

He went back to the yard. Everything seemed to be as it had been, and yet a taut expectancy held him. He stood quite still, his face thoughtful, his eyes narrowed to blue-gray slits. No movement. No sound. Only the dull fly-drone of after-noon. He walked across to the stock sheds—rude buildings of upright cottonwood posts with pole and hay roofs. There again—the glint of cartridges.

"Heads!"

He said the word unexpectedly. Perhaps it even surprised himself. He spun, drew, fired, all in one careless movement. There was no snake. One of the empty cartridge cases leaped from the ground and buzzed for fifty feet, coming to rest against a clump of hoof-tramped sage.

He laughed easily to himself, blew smoke from the gun, and reloaded it quietly. Shooting had snapped the tight feeling of repression that had settled over him. It affected him like whiskey might another man.

He no longer felt that someone was watching him. He walked in his spavined cowboy manner across the yard, remounted, and retraced his way back to the herd.

"Snake?" Big Jim asked, referring to the shot.

"No, just *bang*. I don't like quiet places."

Big Jim jerked his head in disgust. He could go for weeks on end without feeling compelled to burn a cartridge, while Hernandez and the Kid were blasting them by the boxful.

The Kid went on, speaking softly: "Shootin' seems to be in style here in Montana Territory, anyhow. If you're in doubt of that, my three-ton friend, just go down and see what they did to the poor old Two Bar."

Another search of the place revealed nothing. Only more empty cartridges out in the sagebrush. It looked as if somebody had put up an all-night stand.

The Pecos Kid rode off, musing: "You know, I heard that Dermott was having himself some trouble over this Mandan Springs country. And Carson down in Cheyenne said there was plenty of money due to grow out of this ground once the Northern Pacific Railroad pushed her rails in from Dakota Territory."

"*This* ground?" Big Jim asked, looking at the baked gumbo.

"It doesn't look anything extra as a cow country, does it? I wonder what in hell was worth shooting about down there."

The Pecos Kid was unusually thoughtful all the while they moved the herd to one of the springs that made a green splash of color along the descending benches.

Hernandez, noticing his preoccupation, said: "I theenk it

15

is that girl across the tracks in Dodge. The girl who would have been mine had she not seen your pink hair, *señor*. Is she the one you dream of, Keed?"

"No. I was thinking about Dermott and the million-dollar proposition he's supposed to have for us. And I was just wondering how many we'd end up by ducking ourselves."

"Bullets, *poof!* The lead bullet is the national flower of Chihuahua. The coat of arms of my family, *señor* . . . one bullet hole rampant on the upside-down sombrero. And the motto . . . 'Shoot first and talk afterward.' "

Big Jim grumbled: "I'll end up by buryin' both of you."

It was almost dark when their supper of salt pork and flapjacks had been cooked on a tiny fire amid box elder brush.

"You stand the watch as usual," Bill Warren said to Jim. "On foot. Just hunker in the brush with your Winchester. I don't want some bushwhacker knocking you off."

For a long time after lying down in his tarp and blanket, Bill Warren watched the sky overhead through the box elder leaves. He fell asleep without realizing it, and awakened suddenly as Big Jim prowled in at the end of his watch.

"Nothing?"

"Didn't hear a thing."

Warren dressed, drew his Winchester from its scabbard, followed the hoof-punched mud along a tiny stream leading down from the springs. Away from brush shadow, things were sharply revealed by the moon's strong highlight and shadow.

He moved carefully beyond the bushes, climbed a low knoll, and sat in the shadow of a sagebrush cold-smoking a cigarette. The cattle seemed a trifle restless. One cow, three or four hundred yards away, was up and bawling. He flipped the cigarette away.

Gunfire came in a concerted rattle, sending pencils of

flame from the side of a dry wash. Warren instinctively brought up the Winchester, but the shooting was far out of range. An instant later riders appeared, single file, racing from the dry wash, shouting and firing to stampede the cattle.

The rest happened with amazing rapidity. Instantly the herd was up and on the move. It was as though every animal had been crouched and waiting, instead of bedded for the night.

For an instant they seemed headed for the camp, but they ran parallel with the creek straight for the maze of coulées and dry washes that make up the Yellowstone badlands. Dust rose, and here and there he could still glimpse the red flare of burning powder.

He ran down, past the springs. Big Jim was bellowing.

"It's me," Warren said, glimpsing gun shine.

"What in hell?"

The hoofs were a diminishing rumble. No shooting now. Big Jim located his hobbled horse. Too late, by the time he'd freed the animal. Night air that had been sharp and clean was now choking full of heavy dust.

"Keed!" Hernandez said.

"Here I am."

"Ha!" Hernandez's teeth showed in the dark. "At least, I have the good fortune to be relieved of my morning watch. You theenk perhaps it is rustlers? There is nothing your dear Hernandez Pedro Gonzales y Fuente Jesús María Flanagan would rather do than go on the hunt for those two-legged wolves, the rustlers."

"Rustlers be damned! No rustler would be dull enough to drive cattle in the breaks where it'd take two weeks to round them up."

"Ah, so. Then you theenk it is the enemies of our dear employer that we have never met, thees *Señor* Moneybags whose dirty *gringo* name I have forgotten?"

"Dermott? I don't know. I don't know whether he has any idea what's going on out here or not. But I intend to ride in to Miles Town tomorrow and find out."

# II

# "GUNMAN'S TOWN"

Daylight. They followed the churned ground of the stampede and sat for a while, scanning intricately eroded country in the direction of the Yellowstone. Half an hour later Hernandez located the tracks of saddle horses, heading across bench country to the east.

Six horsemen. Perhaps seven. They made no particular effort to make sure. After eight or nine miles one of the sets of tracks quit the rest and struck out cross-country toward Miles.

Bill Warren jerked his head indicating they'd follow the lone rider's tracks.

"Follow *one* of 'em?" Jim blurted.

"I'd rather swap bullets with one man than five," the Pecos Kid said with great seriousness. "It's safer."

For mile after mile the Pecos Kid rode in silence, watching the hoof marks of the lone horsemen as they disappeared and appeared again on the hard-baked gumbo of the prairie. He was thinking about this job he'd taken. There was something peculiar about it. He'd thought so from the first when Wallace Carson, the wholesale merchant in Cheyenne, had hired him in the name of Roger Dermott of Miles Town to drive a herd of cattle northward to the Yellowstone.

Three hundred dollars would have been generous enough pay for the three of them. Instead, Wallace Carson had paid over five hundred and promised him that Dermott would

19

have an unusual proposition for him when the drive was completed.

"There are big things happening along the Yellowstone, what with the Northern Pacific on its way from Bismarck," Carson had said. "Dermott needs a man like you. He has a proposition that will make you one of the big men of the Northwest."

The idea of himself, Bill Warren, the Pecos Kid, late of the Confederate cavalry and later of more places than he could remember, being one of the *big men of the Northwest* amused him. He laughed about it now.

Hernandez was at one side, slightly behind. Something he did telegraphed his intention, and the Pecos Kid turned, drawing at the same instant. But Hernandez's cross-draw was ahead of him, and the snake was left writhing and headless.

"Heads!"

Warren checked himself with his thumb hooked over the hammer. "Tails," he said sadly, taking a long bead to cut the rattles off.

"And now, *señor,* I am pleased to tell you that I owe you only forty-nine thousand and nine dollars!"

The sun had set, when they reached Miles. Lights were burning here and there in a saloon or dance hall. The hoofs of countless saddle horses had pulverized the gumbo of Front Street until it was fine and grayish white, like unbleached flour. After the hard prairie it was like riding across a featherbed.

They reined in before the Apex Livery Stable and sat for a while, stiff and tired from a day in the saddle. At last a half-breed boy came from inside. Warren got down then, tossed him the reins, and limped around, kicking the stiffness of long travel from his legs. He started limping away and paused fifteen or twenty steps away on one of the platform sidewalks.

"I'm going to hunt out Dermott," he said, addressing Hernandez, "and you lay off the high wine till I get back. You just lost a herd of mighty fine stockers for the gentleman, and, if he wants your story as well as mine, I'd like to have you sober enough to give it."

"You have ever seen me drunk, *señor?* Me? Hernandez Pedro Gonzales. . . ."

"I said to stay sober, or so help me I'll part that wavy black hair of yours with the barrel of my Forty-Four." He pointed to Big Jim and said: "That goes for you, too. I'm sick of getting you out of jams. If you get in one tonight, you can go out feet first, and the hell with you!"

"And the hell weeth you, too, *señor!*"

A batwing door flapped as he walked by, and the Kid caught the stale odor of beer. A grin broke the lines of his face, when he thought maybe he'd have a hard enough time keeping himself clear of the whiskey dumps, let alone worry about anyone so eminently able to care for himself as Hernandez Flanagan.

It was growing dark, but there was still enough light to reveal a warehouse sign down by the river docks reading: **Dermott & Co., Freight**. A jerkline mule outfit had been pulled up to the loading platform, and the driver directed him to some outside stairs that led to Dermott's office.

There was a short length of hall, a door. He rapped without getting an answer. No light. Dermott obviously wasn't there. He cursed through his teeth. He was in a hurry to find Dermott. That lone horseman headed to Miles—it could mean nothing, but it troubled him.

He went outside, found the Carson Brothers' Store, asked for him there. They directed him to the express office. Dermott had not been there since late that afternoon. He had no reason to suppose the lone horseman had ridden in to kill

Dermott. Yet the hunch was there, growing inside him.

He found the marshal—a long, lean man by the name of Wells. He shook his head at mention of Dermott's name. He didn't seem to care a damn whether Warren found him or not.

"Look for him tomorrow."

"What if he happens to get bushwhacked tonight?"

"Well, what if he does?"

Not everyone in Miles worried about Dermott's health.

He was passing a Chinese café. He stopped abruptly. A man sitting inside seemed familiar. He was lean and hunched with big hands dangling at the ends of skinny, long arms. He must have felt Warren's gaze, for he whirled around and stood with the thumb of his right hand hooked in his pants just above the butt of a Colt revolver.

Warren knew him by some mannerism of his movement, even before seeing his long, slack-jawed face. The gunman— Eldad Stark. He carried two guns, low and tied to his legs with bits of whang leather. The strings made his legs look skinny and his gray cotton pants too big for him.

"Well, I'm damned," said Stark. "It's the Pecos Kid."

"Who you riding for these days, Stark?"

Stark lacked a well-rounded intelligence, but there was a weasel quality about him, and he was sharp enough to catch the sarcasm in Warren's question.

"I take care of my business. And as far as that goes, you never was one to put many saddle boils on *your* rump, either. If you have an idea of ringing me in on that Arkansas River business, I'll tell you this . . . I was in Dodge, working for Sam Black."

Bill Warren had spent four months of the past year working for the Arkansas River Stockman's Federation, running down a band of cattle raiders, whites and half-breeds

22

who'd disguised themselves as Comanches.

"You're too quick for me." Warren watched him with eyes that were narrow and hard as slits of blue-gray quartz. "I never thought you had anything to do with it."

No, Stark would never fool with anything that involved so much work as cattle raiding, but the Kid didn't say so. Stark was afraid of him, but he'd go for those low-slung guns rather than take any abuse in public. Pecos wanted no fight with the man right now.

Stark swaggered a little and said: "All right, then." He leaned against the building so he could see Warren and down the street both. By his attitude it was obvious he was waiting for someone. His right hand stayed nervously above his gun.

"Who you waiting to bushwhack, Eldad?" Warren asked.

"I don't bushwhack."

"You didn't just ride into town, did you?"

Stark was looking at him beneath droopy eyelashes. His slack jaw moved, and he was smiling a little.

Pecos went on: "You didn't ride in from Mandan Springs way on a lame horse to put a slug through Roger Dermott?"

Stark laughed, and it sounded genuine. "Why, Kid. Ain't you heard? I shouldn't tell you this, but it's too good to keep. Us, me and you, we're on the same side of this fence. Sure, I work for Dermott, too."

Pecos stood for a while, thinking it over. "How did you know I was working for Dermott?"

"He told me. Right after you rode into town."

"He knows I'm here?"

"Dermott keeps pretty close tabs on things in Miles. He knows you're here, all right."

"Where is he?"

Stark shrugged his loose shoulders. There was something down the street now occupying his attention. That nervous right hand had stopped. A woman had come from the front door of a two-story frame building called **Johnny's Round Tent** and was walking toward them along the platform sidewalks.

She was taking her time, apparently waiting for somebody to see her. Pecos knew she was part of the play—part of Eldad Stark's play.

A third party took his place. This was a tall, young man, a cowboy, who walked from the door of a general store and was looking across at her. The tall, young man started to cross the street. Stark had gone lax, his arms long and loose.

"Stark!" Pecos shouted.

Sound of the gunman's name made the young cowboy spin around. He saw Stark then by sidelight from the Chinese café. He realized instantly that the gunman had been placed there to kill him.

He stepped back. For an instant it seemed that he was going to reach for the six-gun on his hip. He didn't. He got his hands high, hooked the door behind him with his spur, opened it, went back inside.

"Stark, you got a match for my cigarette?" Pecos asked in soft amusement.

The woman had stopped and was looking across the street at them. She had a soft, dusky loveliness—no ordinary dance-hall girl even though she had come from the Round Tent.

Stark said: "Do you know . . . ?"

"I know I don't like deadfalls."

Stark remained for a moment, looking at him with savage eyes, then he turned and slouched down the street.

A couple of freighters came from the Chinese café, picking their teeth. "Who was he?" Pecos asked, jerking his head at the tall cowboy.

"One of them tough Barbour boys from Mandan Springs.

24

He's in here chasing Lona Pearl again. Hoss Barbour would break his neck if he knew." He appraised the woman and muttered: "Not that I blame him."

Pecos glanced at the woman again. So she was Lona Pearl. It was easy to see why men were still talking about her when they got as far away as Dodge. She had a round, full beauty that hit a man hard.

She was looking at Pecos. Still watching him, smiling a little, she stepped down from the platform sidewalk and picked her way across the soft dust of the street.

"Hello, boy," she said.

Bill Warren was twenty-eight, with three years of the Civil War and ten years of frontier trails and boom towns behind him, but there was something that made those camp-following women grow wistful when they saw his face. That woman in San Saba had called him "boy," too, and there was that blonde girl across the tracks in Dodge.

Lona Pearl came close, and he was conscious of her subtle, New Orleans perfume.

"Boy, why don't you speak to women?"

Pecos grinned and said: "Is it safe?"

She laughed, knowing he was referring to the deadfall that she and Stark had set for that tall Barbour fellow. She was the sort of woman who would enjoy seeing a man die for her.

"Why don't you see me at the Round Tent?" she asked, tilting her head at the two-story dance hall down the street.

"How about Johnny Malette?"

She was Johnny's girl—Johnny Malette, the riverboat gambler who had lighted in Miles and built the Round Tent.

"You're afraid of him, *M'shu?* I thought the Pecos Kid was afraid of nothing."

Everyone seemed to know him in Miles Town. It's not easy to ride off and leave a reputation after once you've

25

blazed it out. She walked away, smiling over her shoulder. There was a swaying motion about her that was an invitation.

So Dermott knew he was in town, and Dermott was able to take care of himself. The Pecos Kid decided to have that cold bottle of St. Louis beer.

A wrinkled old Chinese was blocking his way, when he turned. He was holding a slip of paper covered with Chinese characters—a lottery ticket.

"Fifty cent? Win fifty dolla?"

A four-bit piece caught light from one of the windows as he flipped it over.

"Does Roger Dermott hang out at Johnny Malette's Round Tent?"

"Yah. Plenty much." He was at work on the ticket, dabbing saliva-ink over certain of the Chinese characters. He handed it over, grinning harder than ever. "You lucky. Red hair lucky. Maybe you win hunna dolla. Two hunna dolla."

"Don't break yourself, John."

He put the lottery ticket away and clomped inside a bar. He was there when Big Jim Swing rushed in and said: "You better come down to the Round Tent."

"Have a beer."

"No. Listen, Kid, Butch has got hold of the tiger's tail for sure this time."

"That Spanish-Irish half-breed can take care of himself. Who's the woman . . . Lona Pearl?"

"You already heard?"

"No, I'm just a good guesser."

# III

# "THE LONE RIDER"

Pecos stopped at one end of the crowded bar in the Round Tent and asked for St. Louis beer. He looked around, studied the room. The saloon and gambling house were in one section of the building; there was a wide arch, and beyond a combination theater and dance hall. Only a couple of lamps were burning. A fiddler was tuning up.

The ceiling of the dance hall was lower than the saloon, and a balcony had been cut through with stairs that led directly from the saloon to its second story. A man was sitting up there, keeping to shadow, tilted against the wall. After a time he moved, scratched. It was Eldad Stark.

Deadfall. The more he looked at things here in Miles, the less he liked working for Roger Dermott.

"There's Tom Barbour!" a man said near him.

He whirled. Tom Barbour, the tall cowboy, had come in the room. Pecos had his first good view of him as he stood looking flushed and sharp-eyed around the room. He was about twenty-one, and, if a person didn't know, he'd have taken him to be one of those Easterners who came West to heal their diseased lungs.

Barbour saw Lona. He became eager, almost smiling. He pushed through, never taking his eyes from her.

A hushed expectancy settled over the room. Men edged away, wary for trouble. Lona was smiling with a soft, feline quality. She moved with a slight sway of her body, half circled the table, stopped with her eyes on Tom Barbour's face. Barbour reached as though expecting her take his hand. She didn't.

"Lona. Come here."

She laughed. A dulcet sound.

"Lona. I want to talk to you."

"But do I want to talk to *you?*"

"But last week you said. . . ."

"I have said many things. And I have changed my mind. Tonight I do not want to see you."

His face went hollow. He said something through his teeth. Perhaps he cursed her. Pecos wouldn't have blamed him. She was deliberately building the thing to a shoot-out. Barbour started forward.

She moved, but only a little. "Don't touch me!" She flung herself against the wall, looked back at the table she had left.

Pecos started. Her companion there was Hernandez Flanagan. The Irish-Mexican's eyes were glittering with sardonic amusement. He smiled slowly. "You weel leave the girl alone, *señor!*"

Barbour did not seem to hear him. He came another step, but Lona still avoided him. She pretended to be weeping. Barbour moved closer to her.

"Leave her alone!" Hernandez rapped out.

Barbour for the first time took notice of Hernandez. "You stay out of this! I ain't takin' anything from any damned greaser."

Hernandez was smiling. There was a tense, glittering quality about it that Pecos recognized.

"Butch!" the Kid shouted.

Tom Barbour had turned to face Hernandez. His feet were spread; he'd rocked to a half crouch; his right hand was poised and tense. It was a gunfighter's pose, but his Colt was too far back on his hip, its butt too flat with his body. He'd be no match for the deft, cross-draw that those Chihuahua aristocrats start learning at the age of six.

There was a bare half second of hesitation. Then Barbour spun aside with his hand raking upward. Men stampeded. Pecos was already hurling a heavy oak chair. The chair struck Hernandez shoulder high, its unexpected weight driving him to the wall. His gun, already out, exploded, sending wild flame across the heads of the crowd.

Pecos was diving forward even as Barbour hurled the chair. He smashed Barbour's gun from his hand at the same instant it cleared the holster. The Kid's weight carried the taller man to the wall.

Barbour's head snapped back and struck hard. Stunned, he fell forward. Pecos wheeled to a crouch. His gun was drawn, angled toward Eldad Stark in the balcony.

"Drop it!" Pecos said.

Stark was crouched, his left-hand pistol drawn. His face was slack and savage. He hated Warren—he'd always hated him. He'd been waiting up there to get Barbour in the back, but he'd gladly have blasted Bill Warren instead.

Stark looked for a few seconds down the black muzzle of Warren's .44. He shrugged and slid his own gun back in its holster.

"Johnny don't want trouble around here," Stark said lamely.

A man had picked up Tom Barbour's gun. Pecos took it and punched out the cartridges. Barbour was up but groggy. He looked at Pecos and snarled: "Damn you!"

"He just saved your life, cowboy," a short, middle-aged man said.

Pecos gave him the gun. "Don't try to load it."

Barbour was still cursing, but he put the gun away as it was.

"You know him, Bolton," somebody said. "Get him his horse and start him out of town."

Bolton was a blond cowboy about Barbour's age. He said: "His horse is lame."

The words struck the Pecos Kid like a jolt to the face. He looked at Barbour and remembered what they'd said about "those rough Barbour boys from Mandan Springs."

Tom Barbour was the lone rider they'd been following. And he'd saved the man's life. He laughed and walked back to the bar.

# IV

## "DERMOTT"

Barbour was gone, and Pecos was halfway through his second bottle of beer when a Negro came up, touched the bill of his stiff-billed steamboat cap, and said: "Mist' Warren, seh. A gentleman would like to see you. Upstairs."

"Who is he?"

"Mist' Dermott."

The name brought Pecos up in a hurry. He clomped down the bottle and followed. At last he was to meet Roger Dermott face to face.

The Negro led him across the balcony, down a short hall, rapped at a gilded door.

"Come in!" said the voice of Lona Pearl.

She stepped back, silhouetted by lamplight, smiling at him. Pecos went in. The room was luxurious. In the center stood a table of Caribbean mahogany, carved after the Cuban fashion. A chair had been placed for him. There were glasses and a decanter of something that looked like sherry.

"Drink it, boy?" she asked.

It was a Portuguese brandy with a sweetish taste—sickening after beer.

She said: "You're afraid of me, boy?"

"Leave him alone, Lona," a man said. He walked into the room. "I'm Johnny Malette."

Johnny Malette was medium in height and weight, about thirty-five years old, muscular, graceful. His skin was dark,

31

hair almost black, thick, and combed in a pompadour. Despite the warmth of the room he wore a coat and vest. No gun in sight. It would be carried gambler style in an armpit holster.

They shook hands, and Malette said: "Well, it isn't often one finds a major of cavalry in this water hole of hell."

"I thought this was an Army post." Pecos was referring to Fort Keogh across the river.

"Union Army!"

"Why, yes. Isn't that the only Army left? I'm sorry, Malette, but I stopped fighting the war eight or nine years ago."

"I suppose that's a good enough attitude . . . but I can't help hating the yellow guts of those Yankees who grab the range and let you Texas boys eat the dirt off the drag."

"Tom Barbour sounded like a Texas boy."

Johnny Malette's face went hard. "Why'd you say that?"

"I know you had a deadfall set. Maybe that's your business. But after this, furnish your own triggers, and don't drag my boy Hernandez in on it."

Malette stood quite still. His fingers, long, manicured and dead-looking, rested on the edge of the table. "You're my guest," he said.

"That word only applies among gentlemen."

Dermott had a firm step. He came in and stood for a moment, looking in Warren's face. He was powerful, about thirty-five, and his eyes, at that moment, seemed to have the power of seeing into a man's mind. What he saw in Warren's seemed to please him. He said: "Warren, I'm damned glad to meet you."

"Not after you hear about those cattle at the Two Bar."

"I already heard, and I'm still glad to meet you. You don't need to tell me about the Two Bar. Those gunmen spent all night trying to get Prescott, but he was out in the coulées when they stampeded the cattle. In a way I'm glad they did it, because now you know what I'm up against." He lifted the brandy. "Have you ever heard of the Northern Pacific land grant?"

Warren nodded. There'd been much public attention centered on the Northern Pacific land since Black Friday, and the failure of Jay Cooke and Company, and the scandal revolving around the Credit Mobelier. The Credit Mobelier was a money-raising agency of the Union Pacific which had apparently insinuated itself a little too closely to the government moneybags. Although the N.P. had escaped scandal, there'd been considerable scrutiny of the forty-seven million acres of land that the railroad had been given on each side of its right-of-way.

Dermott went on. "I'm a businessman. I know what will happen to steamboat transportation when the Northern Pacific shoves its rails west from Bismarck. The Dermott steamboat line will be through. Horse-drawn freight will hang on for a while. Maybe a dozen years, each year less profitable. I can't fight the railroad. It will develop the country, and, if I make my investments wisely, I'll develop along with it.

"It was with this in mind that I purchased my options on certain N.P. sections. Some of them happen to cover the area around Mandan Springs. The springs follow low ground roughly parallel with the Yellowstone, cropping up here and there on a flat valley floor. Naturally they attracted settlers. The settlers have no title to the land, but they've built shanties, corrals, a few things like that, and they're running cattle.

"I have the right to put them off, but I don't care to get myself a bad reputation. I made an offer to purchase all the improvements. Offered to freight everything free of charge up north to the Musselshell. But the settlers got together and formed what they call the Mandan Springs Protective Association. They're fortified at Cap Coyne's ranch now. Frankly, I think Cap would be willing to compromise, but the Barbour boys are shouting damn' Yankees, and all the old Rebs want to fight Pea Ridge all over again."

Bill Warren said: "If it's only a long term investment, I'd sit tight."

Roger Dermott laughed and stopped looking at his blunt fingers. "I've been sitting tight. Now they've taken to sniping at my steamboats. There's no way of patrolling the river, even if the Army didn't have its hands full, watching Sitting Bull. On its way up, the *Western Enterprise* was fired on, and one of the bullets came within a single inch of striking Missus Thad Nolan of Bozeman. She was in her stateroom, and it broke the water pitcher she'd just put back on the stand. The *Red Cloud* had three windows torn out of her pilot house while she was hung up on a sandbar at the Wilkes Crossing."

"Sure they weren't Indian bullets?"

"I'm not sure of anything. All I'm sure of is that I started having trouble with the Barbour boys, and my steamboats started getting riddled at the same time." Dermott got to his feet with a sudden movement and stood with hands thrust in pockets, fists doubled, drawing his cross-weave riding trousers tight. "Damn it, man, I've always believed in direct action. When a man shoots at me, it's been my policy to shoot back. Sitting still in the middle of this row is the hardest thing I've ever had to do."

"And so you sent for me," Warren said. "It's too bad that I'm not a traveling gun hawk. When Carson talked to me in Cheyenne, he said you had some sort of a *business* proposition. I'm like you. I'd like to take root somewhere and grow. I have a couple of friends, too."

"I'm not interested in the gun at your hip."

"No?"

"Gunmen are thirteen to the dozen. I'm not going to start shooting unless I have to."

"So what am I to do?"

"I want you to go out there for me. You're a Texan. You were once an officer under Johnston. Maybe they'll listen to you. It's as much for their good as it is for mine."

"Just *what* do you want me to do?"

"Tell them I'll pay for all the improvements they've put on the land."

"*Their* valuation?"

"Senator Reeves is coming out here next month. . . ."

"Carpetbagger Reeves?" Warren asked wryly.

"I don't intend to argue his qualifications for office. He's a United States senator, and he's coming here representing the Committee on Public Lands. I'm willing to let him arbitrate the price. If you can't get them to accept my offer, at least prevent them from attacking my boats. If they have anything drastic in mind, I'd like to know about it in time to fight it."

"And that business proposition you mentioned?"

"Carson and myself are incorporating under the title of Northwest Mercantile. It's inevitable, I suppose, that a concern like ours would get in the cattle business on a pretty far-flung basis. I can't think of anyone who could better manage it than yourself. You and those two friends you ride with. If you carry this thing through successfully, I'm willing to write you down for a five percent share of our capital stock. I hope you realize how much that would amount to." Dermott waited. "Well?"

"I'll tell you tomorrow."

# V

# "THE J BAR O BOYS"

It was evening when the Pecos Kid, Hernandez Flanagan, and Big Jim Swing drew their horses to a halt on rimrock overlooking the long valley that bore the name Mandan Springs. This was where the Barbour boys and Cap Coyne were forted up.

Streams wound here and there, their courses marked by dark lines of willow and box elder. Grass was good, but not exceptional. A log cabin and some corrals, built at one of the nearby springs, had apparently been abandoned. About three miles to the north they could see a larger accumulation of log buildings and corrals, and that, they knew, was Cap Coyne's place, the Double C.

They could see a man riding up from a pasture, driving half a dozen horses. Despite distance, the clear, rare atmosphere of the prairie allowed them to detect every move he made when he dismounted, lifted down some gate bars, and turned the horses loose in a corral.

"Peaceful enough." Pecos grinned. "We shouldn't have anything to worry about, after saving young Barbour's hide. They'll probably butcher the fat cow when we get there."

"What ranch we supposed to have bought?" Jim asked.

"The J Bar O. That was the Jaques and Oliver spread. But I'll do the talking."

Pecos touched his spurs lightly, and his tired buckskin

picked a zigzag course through broken rimrock strata to the valley. The trail turned and followed along the side of a dry wash, but Pecos avoided it, choosing instead a bulge of the country where their approach could be plainly marked from all directions.

A needle-sharp reflection came from the side of a knoll, and Hernandez, seeing it, muttered: "Telescope."

"Sure, they have a look-out posted. Didn't Dermott say they'd turned this place into a fortress?"

A man walked into sight, leading a dark pony. He mounted and sat for a while. Other riders appeared from around one of the log bunkhouses. Eight altogether. They headed across the flats, fanning out, and light now and then caught reflections of gun shine from the Winchesters they carried across their saddles.

One of them spurred his horse to a lope and was a couple hundred yards ahead when the Kid got close enough to see his face. He was about forty, big and raw-boned, with an unruly mass of rusty, bristly hair that hung below his collar. He reined in and sat back on his big chestnut horse, legs stiff, and the heels of his choke-bore boots thrust forward, one arm uplifted to shade his eyes against the sunset.

"What ye want?" he bellowed.

He might have been a trapper or mountain man from the style of his greeting, but something in the twist of his words told Pecos he was from Texas.

"You're one of the Barbour boys," he said.

The man had a chaw of tobacco in one cheek, and he took time to work it around for a while. "So I be. Hoss Barbour. But I don't remember you from nowhere."

"I'm Warren." Evidently the name meant nothing to him. "They call me the Pecos Kid."

He moved then, and spat explosively. "I hear tell you

saved that damned fool brother o' mine from a one-way trip to that Miles boothill."

"He was a little bit outnumbered."

"Anybody damn' fool enough to walk inside a deadfall like Johnny's Round Tent deserves to get his lights shot out." Then he softened a little. "But he's the young 'un of us, and we try to look out for him. Anybody that saved his life is welcome to eat my grub and sleep in my bed, and no questions asked." He nudged his pony forward and leaned to one side, shoving his Henry rifle in a scabbard. "You boys driftin' or stayin'?"

Obviously he'd fully expected them to say "driftin'," because he straightened suddenly, and his blue-gray eyes became narrow when Warren answered: "I guess we'll stay a year or three. We just bought up the J Bar O place."

"Damnation!"

"What's wrong? Has somebody jumped the claim?"

"Squatter rights. Long as Jaques and Oliver ain't been gone more'n a year, they can sell to who they please, but I don't reckon you bought yourself more'n a potful of trouble." He motioned for the other men to come on, and in the meantime he poked more cut plug in the side of his cheek. "Maybe we *could* do with three more gun whangers in case you have the stomach for suicide."

"Dermott?"

"They told you, then?"

"They told us."

"It ain't any of my business, but how much did you pay Jaques for that place?"

"Four hundred."

"Four hundred! Sweet land o' hell, if I had four hundred. . . ."

"They say Dermott would pay more than that."

38

"I wouldn't sell to that damn' Yankee for four times four thousand." He proceeded to curse Dermott, naming him every vile term he'd picked up between the Brazos and the Missouri. Suddenly, noticing how close the riders were, he stopped. It seemed strange that a man like Hoss Barbour would not want them to hear his profanity—then Warren noticed the reason. One of those was a girl.

She was dressed in Levi's, boots, a blue shirt, and sombrero, like the rest. Warren might have mistaken her for a remarkably handsome boy were it not for her hair that had been braided, wrapped in close coils around her head, but still was so bountiful it escaped from beneath her sombrero.

When Hoss stopped, Hernandez proceeded to add some south-of-the-border terms of his own before Warren stopped him. "The girl," he said.

Hernandez's eyes became extremely wide. He smiled his pleasure, showing his excellent teeth. He touched his close, dark mustache and seemed to be sorry that his guitar was wrapped in his soogans and roped on the pack horse.

"Stay back!" Pecos growled at him.

Hoss turned and said: "These are the boys that saved Tom's skin last night. Turns out they bought the J Bar O. I reckon that makes 'em one of us if they want to stay."

A lank, lean man, rust-complexioned with a scar-disfigured cheek, rode closer and made a point of keeping his Winchester ready. He was obviously another of the Barbours. "Where did you hail from?" he asked, addressing Warren.

Along the frontier a man's back trail was considered his own affair, and consequently this particular question was one reserved for lawmen and not often asked by them.

Hernandez turned suddenly, an angry motion, but Warren stopped him and said: "I'm the Pecos Kid."

The second Barbour jerked back, grunted. "So. Well,

that's better'n being a damn' Yankee, but don't get the idea you can ride far on that business in the Round Tent last. . . ."

"Zenis!" Hoss barked.

"What do we know about these . . . ?"

"I said they could stay!"

"All right," Zenis grumbled. "The Kid's a Texas man, and I don't object." He was looking at Hernandez. "But I ain't bushin' up with any knife-throwin' greaser. He'd've kilt Tom last night. . . ."

"Shut your mouth!" Hoss shouted. He held a short, coiled bullwhip in his hand. It was too long to be of much use as a quirt, so obviously it was carried as a weapon. He turned on Zenis with the thing shoulder high, but the threat only made his brother look more vicious than ever.

"No, I ain't closin' my trap!"

"You were speaking of me, *señor?*" Hernandez asked softly.

"Yes, I was speakin' of you!"

"Last night your brother called me this thing, and I let him live, for he was young, and a fool. I think you will die, for you are old, and a fool."

Zenis had the Winchester across the pommel. It was a simple matter to lift it, cock the hammer, and fire. Hernandez's hand was already moving to his hip. He flung himself sidewise, spurring his horse with the same movement.

Hoss Barbour roared and came down with the bullwhip. Its lash wrapped itself in quick coils around Hernandez's wrist. He swung back. The gun flew high and thudded to the hard-baked prairie earth. The Kid had drawn, but he kept his gun angled skyward, for Hoss Barbour had placed himself to block the Winchester.

Zenis cursed him and tried to get the gun clear. Hoss

grabbed the barrel, and for a moment they struggled for possession. Then Hoss's superior strength made itself felt. He ripped it from Zenis's hand and swung it, stock forward, in a stabbing motion. Zenis caught part of its force with an upflung arm, but it knocked him loose in the saddle. His horse reared, and Hoss finished the job of clubbing him to the ground.

"I told you before I wasn't takin' your lip!" Hoss yelled.

The horse bucked and sprayed chunks of dirt over the fallen man. Hoss sat, looking down on him, breathing hard through his nostrils.

Zenis stood up, covered with dirt and fragments of dead grass, and commenced wiping blood from behind his left ear. He looked up at Hoss as though he hated his guts, but he didn't say another word.

Hoss Barbour jerked his head at Hernandez and said: "Tell him he better be peaceful, too. I don't like the gunfighter way he's got about him."

"Tell him yourself," Warren said.

The girl spoke, and the soft modulation of her voice was a shock after the raw voices of the men.

"It's you Barbours who are always starting the trouble, and there's no need of it."

Hoss laughed and twisted the bullwhip back in a tight coil. "I ain't goin' to argue with *you*, Miss Mary."

"I'll have you know you're not running this whole show."

"Reckon things would be a heap different if we were . . . a whole heap different!"

The girl proved to be Mary Coyne, daughter of Cap Coyne, elected leader of the Mandan Springs ranchers. He was waiting on the back step of the ranch house, a squat and powerful man, with a broad face surrounded by hair that looked like white silk floss.

Dermott had told something of his history—a former Indian scout, captain of a band of Northern irregulars operating out of Fort Leavenworth during the Civil War. At one time in his life he'd carved out a reputation for drinking and gun play, but the years had quieted him.

"I heard about you saving Tom's skin last night." Cap Coyne's handshake was strong, and there was directness and understanding in his bright blue eyes. "He's a wild kid, and he was on the prod because of that no-account woman, Lona Pearl. I want to thank you for all of us."

Zenis Barbour was listening, and it snapped his brittle temper once more. "Us Barbours can do our own fightin', and we can do our own thankin'. . . ."

"Shut up!" roared Hoss.

Zenis clamped his lean jaw tightly and strode on with his spavined, cowboy legs across the lean-to where he splashed water in a wash dish and commenced scrubbing blood and dirt from his face. It was twilight and quite dark beneath the cucumber vines that shaded the lean-to, but Warren was conscious of his eyes, hawk-like and suspicious.

"Having a little trouble with your boys, aren't you?" Cap Coyne said to Hoss.

"*Fightin'* men are generally a little hard to handle."

There was a significance and bitterness in the remark that no one could miss. Those Texans under the leadership of Hoss Barbour were in the majority by twelve men to eighteen, but they were on the prod, looking for a showdown with Roger Dermott. It was a question whether Cap Coyne could go on handling them.

The division became more apparent as the night went on. They did not even have grub together—Cap Coyne and the Yankees eating in the ranch house kitchen while the Barbours and their Texans took food camp-style from a wagon wheeled up to the door of a bunkhouse.

That night Warren sat in the big, roughly furnished front room of the ranch house with Cap Coyne. Neither man spoke for a while. Hernandez Flanagan had tuned his guitar and was singing one of the sad, rhythmical songs of the Chihuahua *caballeros*. He had a good voice, more Celtic than Latin, and Warren could sometimes spend hours with his eyes closed, listening to him.

"They didn't give you any bargain," Cap finally said, referring to the J Bar O. "You'll have to fight for it to keep it. I don't know why this ground is so damned important to Dermott, what with free land reaching from Cheyenne to Milk River. Maybe you wonder why I just don't pull my picket pin and drag north like Jaques and Oliver did. I sometimes wonder myself." Cap turned and watched as Mary came in the room, carrying two thick pottery cups filled with black coffee. "I guess it's because this spread has took to looking like home."

Mary Coyne had changed from Levi's to a fringed, brown riding skirt. It buttoned tightly around her waist, accentuating her slimness, but making her look older than she had looked earlier in the evening. Warren guessed her age at about twenty.

He felt her eyes on him, but, when he looked up, she quickly diverted her gaze. "Canned milk?" she asked.

"No, ma'am."

There was something about her, something he hadn't found on Front Street in McKetrick or across the tracks in Dodge. She was browned by wind and sun, lithe from hard riding. Her shirt sleeves were rolled up, and he could tell by the supple fullness of her arms that she'd been raised to do the work of a man.

Cap Coyne was still talking, but Warren's thoughts had

traveled far back to Texas and that other girl, the girl who had promised to wait. It would have been easier if she hadn't *waited,* but she had. She had been there for him to take, the day he had ridden back after the futile weeks of guerrilla fighting that followed Appomattox—had ridden back ragged and dusty, his horse limping, his cutlass thrown away and one of Sam Colt's new .44 pistols strapped in its place.

He'd hired a rig, and they'd driven out to the old ranch at Liveoaks the next morning. His mother had died during the first year of the war, and his father, lying about his age, had joined up and died of Yankee lead at Pea Ridge. And now the old home was in ruins, with cattle hunting shade in what had once been a drawing room, and everything valuable carted away by a lawless gang of former slaves who were encamped on Junction Creek. Nothing was left.

It was impossible, of course. The world that he knew had crumbled and could never be rebuilt again. He'd talked her into visiting relatives at New Orleans and promised to come for her "when he got on his feet." She'd written, something about another man. He got to counting the years. Eight—nine of them.

"Your coffee!" he heard Mary Coyne say.

Warren took the cup and noticed that Cap Coyne was looking at him. "How was that again? I guess I was dreaming."

"I said you'd probably see eye to eye with Barbour and his crowd, being you're from Texas. All the other Texans have."

"I didn't ride up here to cut any Yankee notches in my pistols. What do they want to do, those Barbours?"

Cap Coyne didn't answer the question directly. "They're a rough crowd," he said. "I guess they've been shoved around too much. I feel like bushwhacking a fat money-grabber now and then myself."

"Dermott?"

44

"Sure. Dermott. And those Carson boys . . . if they ever got close enough."

"Why?"

The word seemed to touch Cap Coyne like a hot iron. "Why? I'll tell you. Because they have us against the wall, and they're strangling us. We have cattle on the range. Grass-fat. Cattle aren't high, but there's always a market for these northern grassers. We'd get by, but his boats won't carry them. Prior commitments, he says . . . yet not one in five of his boats is loaded."

"You could drive to Deadwood."

"Through Sitting Bull's country? Our beef would end in a Sioux kettle and our hair on their *coup* sticks. That leaves Cheyenne on the U.P., and what would we have left after driving across Wyoming? Hide, bone, and tendons like the worst Texas grassers. We decided to sit tight. Now Carson's cut off our credit. Without cash we can't buy a sack of tobacco. It's not easy keeping the boys in line. It's not just Hoss and his Texas crowd. All the boys are getting ringy. They'll cut loose one of these days, and maybe I'll be right in there beside 'em."

In the morning, Warren and his two companions saddled fresh mounts from their saddle string and set out downvalley for the old J Bar O Ranch. They found a one-room cabin of bleached cottonwood logs, a corral, a stock shed with a hay roof. Twenty-five or thirty longhorns wearing Barbour's brand ranged across the bottoms.

The ranch lay at the eastern end of Mandan Springs. Beyond were some low hills, and the descent toward the Powder River country. In the north, four or five miles of benches and badlands, and then the Yellowstone, making intricate patterns through the mudbars of midsummer.

They looked around for an hour, saw little of interest, sprawled in the shade of a box elder tree through the direct sun of afternoon, returning to the Double C an hour past supper time.

"You'll have to take leavin's," old Jack Snow, the cook, told them.

They sat on the back steps and ate from tin plates. Through darkness men kept walking up from the bunkhouses and going in the front door of the big, log house. Little talking. Just a few low words, the thug of boots, jingle of spurs.

Warren put his tin plate aside and stood up. "There's a meeting yonder, and seeing I'm a landholder now. . . ."

"You do not wait for the invitation?" Hernandez asked, smiling.

"It hasn't been my habit in the past."

"I don't like this," Big Jim said. His honest face looked troubled. "I'd like to know who in hell we're sidin' in this row. If it's Dermott, or if it's these Mandan Springs boys."

"We'll see which side will make us the most money." Warren grinned.

"That ain't been your side in the past."

"I've reformed."

Warren clomped through the kitchen. He stopped for a second by the closed door that led to the big, front room. He saw movement in the shadow. Mary Coyne was descending the stairs from the second story. She was looking at him in a certain way, and he knew she thought he was eavesdropping.

"You can't blame one man for listening when the other man whispers," Warren said.

He opened the door for her, but she shook her head and stayed part way up the stairs, so he went inside by himself. He stood with hands resting behind him, closing the door. The room was close from the heat of men, tobacco smoke. The grease dip burned low and reddish as though the press of their bodies tended to absorb the light and steal oxygen away from it.

A rugged man of twenty-five or so had been talking. He stopped. There was a few seconds of silence. Then Zenis Barbour stood up, looking tall and predatory.

"I didn't know anybody asked you to come here, Kid."

"Nobody asked me. We all make oversights. Don't apologize." He had an easy manner that asserted itself during taut moments like these. He kept smiling as though some thought in his own mind amused him. His hands were occupied in rolling a cigarette. "Rode over and looked at my place today. The J Bar O. Liked it first rate. Good grass and water, plenty fresh air, good view of the river. I don't reckon I'll have to drive more'n eight, ten miles once the N.P. lays steel through this country. Can't run much tallow off a critter in eight, ten miles. Lot better than driving clear to Cheyenne across most of hell and all of Wyoming."

"What are you getting at?" Zenis barked.

"Why, just that. The J Bar O will be one of the finest spots north of Red River, if I can hang and rattle till Mister Villard gets that N.P. road built."

"And what'll you do until it gets built?"

"Why, I expect I'll plant a few spuds, and graze some cows, and maybe I'll vary my fare with a catfish now and then out of the Yellowstone. I've heard tell fishing is good down there, if a man has some patience."

"I got patience with fish, but I ain't got patience with wolves. The two-legged kind!"

"Who you mean?"

"Men like Dermott, and the Carson boys, and them that associates with 'em."

Warren did not change expression. He leaned over the

grease dip to light the cigarette, and again, as that night at the Round Tent, his face looked lean and coppery and hard. He was wondering how much Zenis knew and how much simply sprang from the bitter alkali in his system.

"If you think I came here for Dermott, the thing for you to do is say it. Right out. Your intestines ought to be strong enough for that, Zenis. I'm not hostile. And you got backing enough here even if I was."

Zenis spoke: "Sure, I'll say it. I think it was darned funny you'd be with Eldad Stark on Front Street to save Tom's hide the first time, and right handy in the Round Tent when the second play came up."

Warren inhaled and laughed cigarette smoke from his lungs. He sounded genuinely amused. "Now I'll be damned! And every time I ran into him, he was headed into trouble for himself." Tom Barbour was there, sitting against the wall, hunched forward. A big red welt lay across his face, and it was only a guess that Hoss had put it on him with the bullwhip. "Isn't that right, Tom?"

Tom Barbour met his eyes. They looked red and irritated, the way Indians' eyes sometimes become after long sitting in a smoke-filled teepee. He didn't answer.

Warren went on. "I saved your hide at least twice. It's been troubling me ever since. I'm not sure you're worth saving twice in a row. What do you think?"

Tom Barbour's legs uncoiled like twin springs, ramming him to his feet. Hoss told him to stay where he was, elbowed through, and stopped a long stride from Warren, standing with his heavy, choke-bore boots set wide.

"It's like I told you last night. You saved him, and that makes you welcome to eat my grub, ride my horse, or flop in my soogans. But you ain't sitting in on this meeting."

"Why not?"

"You're a newcomer, that's why not."

"And you're afraid I'm a Dermott spy because I went to his office to visit him. Is that right?"

"If I thought you were playin' Dermott's game, I'd blast your insides out. It's a nice, moonlit night outside, Kid. There's a breeze from over the Yellowstone, and, if you get on the right side of the corrals, it smells fine."

Warren looked around. The faces were hostile and suspicious. He laughed, said—"All right, Hoss."—and went outside.

# VI

# "ON THE PROD"

A dark, wiry man stood on the brush-roofed awning with a Winchester across the crook of his arm. He was Blakely, a cowboy from down in the Indian Nations. Warren spoke to him and walked around the house.

Hernandez and Big Jim were still seated on the back steps. Hernandez was talking softly, telling about something from his boyhood back in Chihuahua. Warren stood for a while, feeling the night breeze from across the Yellowstone. Hoss was right about it. It seemed like the farther north a man drifted, the finer those night breezes became.

He turned suddenly and noticed Mary Coyne, standing by the corner.

"You didn't stay long," she said.

"I was taking Hoss Barbour's advice. Fresh air." He flipped his cigarette away and made a motion indicating the badlands and prairie that lay in early moonlight to the north. "Every country has a different smell about it. That, for instance. The muddy Missouri. And maybe the lodge fires of the Blackfeet. I always had a hanker to see the Blackfeet. They must be fightin' men, those Blackfeet!"

"You mean you're getting ready to drift."

"It gets to be sort of a habit."

"What'll you do about the J Bar O?"

"What'd Jaques do?"

"You don't even own it."

He looked at her. There was no use lying. He wondered how much she knew—or guessed. Her eyes were not hostile or suspicious. "I'm not playing Dermott's game," he said.

"I didn't think you were. I only knew you hadn't bought that place from Jaques." Then she asked softly: "Why *are* you here?"

"I don't know." He was being truthful when he said that. He wasn't certain why he'd left the Arkansas, or Dodge, or McKetrick, or all those other places where men of less ability took root and prospered. Money was an excuse. It no longer fooled Hernandez or Big Jim. It had even stopped fooling him. It's not so easy to take hold after a man's roots have been torn up. He gets to looking for something without knowing what it is, and pretty soon he's putting a thousand miles of grass under him, and nothing smells good except the country over the horizon. And so, when the girl asked him, all he could say was that he didn't know. Then he added: "There's some reason Dermott's so set on getting this Mandan strip. What is it?"

"I was going to ask you the same thing."

He noticed that Hernandez had stopped talking about Chihuahua and was listening to them. There was a creak of porch boards when he stood up. "If you ask me, *señorita,* there is gold beneath this earth."

Big Jim snorted. He was from the Mother Lode country of California, and anyone with the most rudimentary knowledge of gold would have known that its presence in these flat prairie sediments would be preposterous.

Hernandez said: "Then, gems. Diamonds. Rubies. Perhaps the water in these springs will make the old man young. *¿Quién sabe?*"

He smiled at Mary Coyne. He looked handsome and debonair despite the two-day's growth of whiskers on his face, but a glance told him that she already preferred Bill Warren. Women always did, and Hernandez could never understand it.

"These northern women," he said under his breath, moving back to sit by Big Jim. "They are cool, *amigo*. The cool blue eyes, the cold yellow hair, they do not have the fire of the women of Chihuahua." He fashioned a long, brown-paper cigarette filled with the strong Spanish tobacco he went to outlandish ends to secure. He inhaled, and the rich smoke seemed to mellow and console him.

"Sure and it's the truth, Jamie, me lad," he went on. His father had been an Irish dragoon, a deserter who ended in Mexico after some fantastic wanderings, and Hernandez could, when he chose, imitate his brogue to perfection. "In faith, Jamie, me bye, there are times when I am tempted to shave off me worthless mustache and burn me guitar for firewood."

"Trouble with you, you're *too* handsome."

Hernandez blew smoke explosively.

"No, it's the truth," Big Jim said. "Women don't like men to be too handsome. They like 'em like the Kid. Freckles and a hammered-up nose and some red hair that won't stay tamed."

"Too handsome!" Hernandez mused, returning to his Spanish accent. "*Sí, mi amigo*. Perhaps you have sometheeng there."

The meeting lasted until almost midnight, with the men grim and brittle-tempered when they came out. Next morning, Warren noticed there was a second powwow inside the Texan's bunkhouse. He walked by and saw that young Bolton was standing near the door.

He was a Northerner, the son of a Pike's Peaker family who had traveled West during the 'Sixties to escape the ravages of Quantrell's raiders, and till that moment he'd considered him one of Cap Coyne's cronies. Evidently Cap's hold on them was slipping.

Big Jim Swing said: "Noticed Lem Barbour in there painting blue on his gun barrel."

"Sure," Warren said. He could guess what had taken place at the meeting. Dermott had pushed them to the spot where it meant fight or get out.

"What do you theenk?" Hernandez asked.

"You're always looking for excitement, and this time it looks like we came to the right spot."

After breakfast, Cap Coyne called the Kid to the front room. A hundred cigarettes were trodden on the floor in evidence of the meeting the night before.

"They're set to go for those steamboats, as you probably guessed already. A dozen snipers and some set snags here and there could raise hell during low water."

"You sound like you'd go along with them."

"I'm not the king of this valley. They elected me captain, but when they swing against you four to one. . . ."

"It'll be the end of you here. All of you."

"You got any better idea?"

"Yes."

The way he said it made Cap Coyne take interest.

"Dermott's not the only boat operator," Warren said.

"You mean the Block R? It operates from a separate warehouse, but Dermott owns it. He and the Carsons."

"I'm talking about Fort Benton. There's Baker Brothers, and Power, and the Gold Line. I delivered a herd to the Two Bar, and the beef boss told me that they charter their own boat and bring it to Liver-Eatin' Johnson's wharf on the Musselshell. If they'll touch there, they'll make the turn at Fort Union and come back here."

"You think we can swing it?"

"I'll start Big Jim overland this morning. Give him that bay long-horse of yours to change off on, and he'll sight Benton by night time, day after tomorrow."

"He can have the pick of my string. I'll go yonder to the bunkhouse and hold some more powwow."

Warren expected trouble with the Barbours, but Hoss gave an ear to the proposition and asked for half an hour to talk it over. It didn't take that long. Inside of ten minutes he came from the bunkhouse with his heavy-legged stride and said: "We'll give you eight days."

"Eight days isn't long enough."

"It's long enough for me. I doubt I could hold my boys longer'n that without hog-tyin' 'em."

# VII

# "FIRE AT FORTY FINGERS"

Jim rode off, mounted on his big roan and leading a pack horse and two extra mounts, the pick of Cap Coyne's remuda. A couple of days passed uneventfully. The second night, Warren groped his way through the open-fronted blacksmith shop to the harness room they were using as sleeping quarters.

"Butch!" he said. It was past midnight by Warren's big silver watch when he walked in. There was mud drying on his boots.

"What'd you see down by the river?" Hernandez asked, guessing where the Kid had been.

"They been sneaking off every night, so tonight I followed. They're fixing an ambush down where the river splits up at a place called the Forty Fingers. Narrow channel. They could raise plenty of hell there."

"Who was there? Zenis? Jib?"

"Sure. And Hoss, too. He'll keep them in line for his eight days."

"And after the eight days?"

"They aren't my steamboats." Warren shrugged.

"You would not even ride to Dermott with the warning?"

"I don't know what I'd do."

Warren lay awake, looking at the blackness of the ceiling for a long time after Hernandez was asleep. There was no clear-cut division between right and wrong here. He neither wanted to help Dermott nor betray the Mandan Springs ranchers, and yet blameless people might die, if they tried to block the river.

Next night Hernandez went scouting. One of the territory's dry rains came up with wind and lightning. Warren walked down from the house and stood in the dark, open front of the blacksmith shop. The wind had a feel of dampness and an odor of freshly wet dust. A man was moving near the corrals. He came up the path, and Warren recognized Hernandez.

"You have seen Mary thees night?" he asked.

"Why, yes, I was just talking to her. What's wrong?"

"Wrong?" Hernandez sighed and kissed his fingers at the black sky. Lightning flashed far away briefly, illuminating his face.

"It was perhaps then a princess of the Blackfeet in love with your Hernandez."

"What the hell are you talking about?"

"That, *señor* . . . a princess, beautiful as the stars of my own Chihuahuas. I only glimpsed her for . . . so long." Hernandez snapped his fingers. "Horseback. A great, black horse, shining from the rain."

"There's been no rain," Warren said.

"Where she came from, there was rain. Did I not see the horse? I called to her, and she rode to the bottom of a dry wash. I thought she would wait for me, but, when I got there, she was gone."

"Pick up her tracks?"

"In this darkness . . . do I have the eyes of a bobcat?"

Next morning they rode out together, but there were the tracks of four horses, mingling, diverging, mixing together again. After a day of intense sun, the storm swung back and once more covered the western sky with cloud banks the color of bullet lead.

With darkness, Hernandez rode out again. Warren

shaved, spent some time puttering with his saddle gear, and walked to the house for the ostensible purpose of securing a piece of beeswax. Mary Coyne was expecting him. He knew that by the starched calico dress she was wearing.

It was a jolt to see her there, so small and slim, and obviously eager to see him. She wasn't the kind for him. She wasn't a girl you kissed and said good bye to. She was the sort you took home with you and kept for good.

But every time he saw her, there would be another vision in his mind, a vision of that girl back in Texas, so he was never quite looking at Mary Coyne. She wasn't the kind for him. His kind were the ones he'd met across the tracks in Dodge. They never brought foolish visions to his mind. They never made his insides turn over from regret.

He should have asked her for the beeswax and left. But he didn't. He stood and talked about things, ordinary things, while he thought of something else. Time went rapidly. He'd been there for more than an hour when the door was flung open unexpectedly and Hoss Barbour stood outside in a gentle drizzle of rain. He started to say something, checked himself. Instead, he clomped inside, leaving blobs of mud, and touched her hair. The action was so unexpected that Mary and Warren only stared at him. He went back and was about to close the door. Then he said: "You ain't been outside lately?"

"No."

He'd been seeing whether her hair was damp from rain.

"Now what the devil?" Warren said, when he was gone.

"He's been having some trouble with Tom."

"Over you?"

"Of course not!"

"I'm sorry. I didn't mean that."

Cap Coyne came in a couple of minutes later. "Hear that

shot?" he asked, without getting too excited about it. "Two or three miles, I guess. Quarter hour ago."

It was raining harder than the Kid had supposed. He stood for a while, hearing its soft hiss as it struck the brush-roofed awning. The dust of the ranch yard was wet to a depth of half an inch over its powder-dry base, and mud clung in clumsy masses to his boots as he crossed to the blacksmith shop. He stopped to listen. There was a commotion down by the corrals. A man raised his voice—Zenis Barbour.

Warren turned and cut diagonally across the shack-cluttered ranch yard, stopping by the roof of a root cellar. The bunkhouse used by the Texans was just beyond.

He could make out the big, rectangular outlines of buildings, but little else. Men were walking up from the corrals. Hoss Barbour said something, and the voice of young Tom Barbour answered.

"You lay that on me again, and I'll kill you, d'you hear?"

The response was sudden. Warren could hear the stamp of struggling men, the grunting exhalations of breath, the jolt of a fist striking bone and flesh.

Hoss panted: "Now maybe you'll tell why you was out there."

"Leave him be, Hoss," Jib said.

Men commenced talking inside the bunkhouse. Someone lighted a lamp. It made an amber glow through the oiled antelope-skin window. Warren circled until he could see the open bunkhouse door fifty or sixty paces away. The Barbour boys came up through the lamplight, four of them, Zenis and Hoss dragging Tom who was wobbly-legged from a blow he'd taken across the jaw. Jib came behind.

"What the hell?" It was Eben Smith, a dark, heavy-shouldered Texan.

"Never mind us Barbours," Hoss said. "We take care of

our own. Git a wash dish full of water."

They balanced Tom in the door and thrust him forward. Tom was erect for a moment with the crown of his Confederate ranger hat almost touching the door casing. Then he reeled forward and would have fallen flat but for a rough-board table.

The others followed inside and left the door open. Warren could have gone closer without much fear of detection, but it would have been useless. The Barbours weren't giving out any information.

He turned and walked to the corral. Bob Guthrie, the night wrangler, was taking care of some horses.

"Now what in hell?" Guthrie said, peering through the gate bars.

"That my sorrel, ramming around?" Warren asked.

"He ain't even in this corral."

Bill Warren knew it. He wanted a glance at Tom's horse. He swung over the corral. It was easier walking through damp manure than through sticky gumbo.

"This Tom's bay horse?"

"Yeah." Guthrie had lined up with the Barbours. He answered the question reluctantly.

Pecos ran his hand down the horse's flank. He'd been ridden hard. There were splashes of mud along his belly and thighs.

Warren climbed back over the corral, and walked to the blacksmith shop.

Darkness was solid inside the shop's smoke-blackened interior. He groped his way by habit around the forge, between the shoe rack and some bags of smithy coal. He stopped, listened. There had been no sound, yet he knew that someone was waiting in the black depths of the shop.

"Who is it?" he said. There was a second or two of silence.

He stepped back, one shoulder against the wall, his Colt lifted from its holster. "Who is it?" he repeated.

"Kid?"

He recognized the voice. It was Eldad Stark. There were certain men that put Warren's nerves on edge, and Stark was one of them. Distaste and contempt and perhaps even a little fear were mixed up in it. He lifted the gun, depressed the trigger to hide the *click-click* sound, and cocked it. Then he answered: "Yes."

"You alone?"

"Yes."

"Better put your gun away."

Stark had heard the slight, metallic sound—that, or seen his silhouette against the dim, red glow from outside. Stark went on: "Sure. Put the gun away. You know I could have killed you, if I'd wanted to. That's a hell of a way to act to a man who's working for the same boss."

Warren lowered the hammer, dropped the gun lightly in its holster. "Who's with you?" he asked.

"How do you know I got anybody here with me?"

"You wouldn't have the guts to come alone."

Stark laughed. It wasn't a pleasant laugh. Darkness did not prevent Warren's knowing what his face looked like—the sideward twist of the slack jaw, the peeling back of his upper lip. "I ain't a damned bit afraid of you, Warren, or of that knife-throwing greaser that sides you. What in hell's the matter with you, anyhow? We're on the same side of the fence, aren't we? Or *are* we?"

"I made a deal with Dermott. If you'd had any part in it, I'd have told him to go to hell."

"Don't shove me too far, Kid," Stark said.

"Why are you here?"

"Dermott sent us."

Warren laughed at the word "us." It was true then, he wasn't alone.

"Who's with you?"

A new voice, guttural and low, said: "Me. The Cherokee Kid."

Warren remembered a heavy, bowlegged man of about thirty-five, dull enough to use his gun for anyone willing to pay him.

Eldad Stark moved forward a little, one boot grating against some iron on the floor. "He wants to know why Jim Swing headed cross-country the other day."

"Jim thinks there's no money in the business, and maybe he's right. What else did Dermott want to know?"

"He's got a hunch there's an ambush being set up down by the river. Do you know anything about it?"

"If there's an ambush, I'll let him know in plenty of time," Warren said.

"You haven't found out anything, then?" The swagger in Stark's voice was indication enough that he was certain Warren was already a traitor to Dermott. When no answer came, he was bold enough to go on. "Maybe that girl at the house has more to offer than Dermott has."

Warren stepped forward, set his heels, and smashed a right toward Stark's jaw. In the dark it landed higher than he'd intended, between cheek and temple. It hammered Stark back. His skull thudded the rough-board wall. He bounded forward, falling, and Warren met him with the other fist.

He was down, groping for his left-hand gun. Warren dropped, pinning him under bent knees. He knew by Stark's movement that he was dragging on his left-hand pistol. He stamped hard, catching the man's wrist beneath the hard instep of his boot. There was a crunching sound of twisting tendon and bone. Stark whined from pain, and his gun thudded on the dirt floor. Warren groped, picked it up, found Stark's second gun pinned in its holster beneath him, and tore it free.

The Cherokee Kid was moving back, and Bill Warren knew his guns were out, although darkness would not let him fire.

"Put 'em back, Cherokee," he said. "They'd just corner you here and kill you."

"What in hell did you do that for?" Stark whined. He was on his knees, clutching his injured wrist. "I came here peaceful. Risked my neck for the boss."

"Get up. If you have any more ideas about that girl, keep 'em to your own lousy mind." He punched the cartridges out on the floor and handed the guns back to him. "What was that shouting half an hour ago?"

"I don't know."

"Did Johnny send Lona Pearl out here to play the moonlight game with that Barbour kid?"

Warren knew by Stark's momentary pause that he'd hit on the truth. "You go back and tell Dermott I'm doing all right," Warren said. "Tell him I'd do a hell of a lot better, if he'd lay the cards on the table."

"What d'you mean by that?" Stark asked.

"I mean about Lona."

"Maybe she did it on her own. Maybe she likes the. . . ."

"Maybe she wants to marry him and settle down in a log shanty and raise kids. That would be Lona's style, wouldn't it?" Warren laughed shortly.

# VIII

# "THE INJUN SIGN"

On the eighth day Big Jim Swing rode back from Benton with word that he'd chartered the Baker Company's old sternwheeler boat, *Rosebud*. It would probably be as far as Fort Union that very day, and back to the landing at Woodhawk's Point by the mouth of the Powder in two more. In anticipation of its arrival most of the men left Cap Coyne's on a beef roundup, an easy job due to the fact that most of the four-year-old butcher stock had been brought in "on the grass" only five or six weeks before. Two days passed, but there was no sign of the boat. It didn't come on the third day, or the fourth.

The following afternoon was still and hot. From the east a column of smoke arose to great height and faded against the sky. There was another column, and another, the last broken into three separate puffs.

Big Jim Swing walked up from the corrals and saw Warren. "Sioux?" he asked.

"I suppose," Warren said. "I hear tell Sitting Bull and the southern chiefs left the agency last month. He's got hell in his craw since that gold strike in the Black Hills."

"And Custer, drinking his wine in Bismarck!"

"Don't blame Custer. He can't fight without men. If the Blackfeet join up, we'll all wish we were in Texas."

Cap Coyne came in time to hear his words. "That's not Sioux smoke."

"Cheyenne?"

Cap shrugged. "It ain't Sioux."

A rider appeared from the northeast and approached, riding swiftly across the flats.

"Hope that ain't one of my horses," Cap said, referring to his speed through the heat of afternoon.

He proved to be Lee Pringle, Eben Smith's nephew. He hurried across to one of the horse sheds, and left a few minutes later accompanied by Zenis Barbour and Eben Smith.

"Maybe they're roundin' up stray cattle," Cap said. "It'd be a good idea with Injun sign in the sky."

Other unexplained arrivals and departures seemed suspicious, too, so, as afternoon faded, Warren saddled and struck across in the approximate direction of the Forty Fingers. The Yellowstone had dropped considerably through the last couple of weeks, leaving mudbars here and there, but its channel was still adequate for steamboat travel. A buffalo trail led across shelf land for a couple of miles, then the hills closed in, and there was a slight climb.

The Pecos Kid drew just short of the low, sage-spotted crest and looked across a widening of the bottoms where the river split in intricate patterns, forming that pilot's perennial nightmare, the Forty Fingers. He found tobacco and papers, twisted up a cigarette, lit it, all without shifting his eyes from the flats below him. A herd of antelope moved across the flats, their tails like white tufts of cotton. They stopped to drink at a backwater. Fresh man-scent would have kept them moving. There was no ambush at the Forty Fingers.

Darkness was settling when he unsaddled at the Double C corrals. He had supper, and then wandered down past the bunkhouses. Old Jack Snow, the Barbours' cook, and Guthrie, the horse wrangler, were sitting on a bench by the door.

"All alone, boys?" he asked.

Guthrie started to answer, but Snow made a movement that stopped him. "I reckon there might be some of the boys asleep inside."

He was lying, of course. Warren laughed in an easy manner, and walked on to the blacksmith shop.

He went inside and lighted the grease-dip. Hernandez and Big Jim had ridden to a woodhawk's trade shanty down toward the mouth of the Powder for tobacco and candy. Big Jim was extremely fond of candy.

Warren pulled off his boots and flopped on the bed which had been left out on the floor. The ranch was the quietest he'd ever known it. Through the glassless window he could hear the musical trickle of spring water flowing through the corrals. The heat of day had vanished, leaving the air cool, filled with the pure fragrance of sage and grasslands.

He dozed—then suddenly he was awake. Lona Pearl! The awareness of her presence was so strong he expected her to be standing there, in the yellow lamplight, looking down on him. The room was empty. He got to one knee in his blankets. Then for the first time he realized what it was. It was the odor of that peculiar French perfume of hers.

Gone now. He tugged on his boots and stood up. A natural wariness kept him from revealing himself at the window with the light at his back. Instead, he moved along the wall and through the door to the blacksmith shop, closing it after him. The shop was dark, with anvil and forge and grindstone making silhouettes against the moonlight outside. He breathed slowly, trying to recapture her perfume, but there was only the stale, ever-present blacksmith shop odor of dead coal and burnt hoofs and rusting iron. It seemed ridiculous, now that he was up and moving around.

He spoke, expecting no answer: "Hello?"

There was movement in the middle darkness, and again

her perfume touched his nostrils.

"Yes, boy," she said. She was picking her way toward him in the dark. It seemed stifling in the airless end of the blacksmith shop. He started forward and drew up when he found her only an arm's reach away.

She was dressed in a blouse, riding skirt, boots. It made her seem smaller than in Miles. Smaller and younger. Her hair had been drawn back and covered by a black silk kerchief.

"Boy," she said, "haven't you anything to say to me?"

"What do you want?"

"Why do you think I'd risk my life coming to see you? Don't you know Johnny would kill me if . . . ?"

"You've been here before," he said. "You were here, seeing Tom Barbour."

"Yes. I was here seeing the young fool." It was too dark to make out her face, but he could imagine the momentary feline expression of distance. "It was nothing."

"Johnny's idea?"

Her hands closed on his upper arms. They were soft and warm and surprisingly strong. "But I am not here to see him tonight. Tonight I am here to see *you*."

It apparently had never occurred to her that there existed a man anywhere who could resist her.

"Did Johnny send you to see *me*, too?" he asked.

Her hands tightened, and he could feel her fingernails burn through the fabric of his shirt. "Of course not. Did I not already say he would kill me if . . . ?"

"Sure."

She'd been expecting him to embrace her. He hadn't, and now his tone brought a sudden, cat-like fury to the surface. She let go his arms and swung the back of her hand at his cheek. One of her rings tore his flesh.

He stepped back, tossing up his hands to protect his eyes. The wall was there, jolting his shoulder. She kept coming. He seized her, and held her at arm's length. She writhed to get free.

It was futile against his strength. At last she stopped. He could sense the rapid rise and fall of her bosom. She spoke, controlling her voice, scarcely a whisper: "Perhaps you do not like Lona!"

"I didn't say that."

"Perhaps it is the girl at the big house. That pale thing with the hair like straw." She waited a second, and went on: "Tell me if you do. Tell me!"

He wished Hernandez Flanagan could overhear their conversation. It would probably be enough to make him fulfill his threat about shaving his mustache and burning his guitar.

"Why do you laugh?" she said.

"Take it easy. I wasn't. . . ."

"Do not think Lona is a fool! She knows what you are doing here. Perhaps I should return and tell Dermott it was *you* who sent for the steamboat! Perhaps I should tell him that you have taken to playing both sides in this business for your own profit. He would kill you! Do you hear? He would kill you. People don't cheat Dermott. Even though you rode ten hundred miles over the horizon, he would send men after you to kill you."

"What made you think I was double-crossing Dermott?" Bill Warren asked.

"I . . . think? I do not think, I know! Johnny Malette, Eldad Stark, the Cherokee Kid . . . these are fools. They would believe anything. But I am a woman. I know when men lie. And you are here, lying to Dermott."

"All right, what are you going to do about it?"

"I lied for you. Listen how I lied for you!" She'd overcome

her anger, and a vibrant eagerness filled her. "I learned things from that fool, Tom Barbour. About the steamboat, about the ambush they are planning tonight by the river."

His face went big-boned and hard, but darkness hid it. He waited, letting her go on.

"These things Lona found out. So easy, a kiss or two. But I did not say to Eldad Stark how I learned. I told him the information came from *you*. Otherwise Dermott would kill you when he learned of the steamboat . . . of the ambush at the Chalk Cliffs tonight. But, instead, you are now trusted as never before. And all because of Lona, after she held your fate like this." He could see the silhouette of her hand, cupped upward, slowly closing. "I could have. But I did not."

The woman was in love with him. He wondered why she'd chosen him from among all the thousands who had moved through Johnny Malette's, west on the great river, north on the long trail from Texas. Tomorrow, it would be someone else. But today it was Bill Warren, the Pecos Kid.

"It wouldn't make any difference to me whether you saved my life or not," he said.

"No?"

"No." His hands closed on her shoulders. He drew her hard against him. For a moment she was a bundle of taut muscle, then she laughed, her hands groped and closed on the front of his shirt, her head was tilted, her lips parted a trifle. It was no great sacrifice to kiss her.

# IX

# "HELL AT THE CHALK CLIFFS"

When Lona Pearl was gone, he started down for the corrals. Jim Swing and Hernandez Flanagan were just leading their horses through the gate.

"We'll have to saddle and ride," he said.

"Sometheeng is wrong?" Hernandez was looking at an extra gun Warren carried.

"Those Texas rawhiders have a deadfall set down by the Chalk Cliffs, and Dermott knows about it."

"Ha! And that ees bad? So let the bushwhackers be themselves bushwhacked, *señor*. I am very sleepy."

"We're riding down there."

"To save Zenis, maybe, and the rest of those *lobos señores!*"

"I'm not worried about the Barbours. This will give Dermott what he's been looking for. He won't stop with them. He'll keep coming. Cap will be next . . . and every poor squatter on these flats."

"Ah, so." Hernandez sighed and hitched up his Colt pistol. "But I would rather sleep in my good bed, *señor.*"

Warren went to rouse Cap Coyne and found the old man fully dressed, sitting in the kitchen, waiting for Jack Snow to brew coffee.

"Sure," Cap said as soon as he saw Warren's face. "I knew they were up to some devilment. Where is it . . . down by the Forty Fingers?"

"The Chalk Cliffs."

Cap strapped on a second Colt revolver, stood on a chair to reach an upper shelf, brought down several cartons of cartridges—.44 Colts and .44-40 Winchesters.

There were only eight others left at the ranch. Apparently all the rest had joined the Barbours. That would give them about twenty-four. Chances were that more had joined from the Box R and the McCabe spread and from the numbers of squatters and wolfers who had stuck to their cabins rather than hole up at the Double C. Forty men might not be a bad guess.

Mary Coyne climbed the corral, sprang to the ground, and walked across with a tinkle of spurs. She was dressed as she'd been when Warren first saw her, and a .32 caliber Smith and Wesson revolver was strapped high around her slim waist.

They set off swiftly, thirteen of them, leaving Jack Snow alone at the ranch. It was not yet midnight when they reached an abandoned squatter's cabin called the Frome place and headed down a steep-sided coulée to the river.

Warren rode up abreast of Coyne and asked how far it was to the Chalk Cliffs. Cap told him it was a couple of miles.

"I been thinkin' about them smoke signals," Cap said. "I told you they weren't Sioux."

"You think Hoss had his look-outs downriver?"

"Sure. Maybe fifty, sixty miles downriver, signaling steamboat. He's no fool, that Hoss Barbour. Dermott better have plenty men because that Hoss'll give 'em one hell of a fight."

For half a mile they followed shelf land through belly-deep sage. There were no sounds except the river current, the soft thud of horses' hoofs.

A gun exploded somewhere upriver. A mile or two. There was the first sharp crack, the rapid clatter of echoes bounding back from hill faces, and a second of silence.

It set off a fury of shooting. Twenty guns—a hundred—it

was impossible to tell with echoes rocketing from the hillsides. Someone spurred to a gallop, but Cap Coyne pulled his horse broadside and shouted: "Hold on. We ain't ridin' into any blind deadfall. We'd git kilt by either side. There's a considerable country down by the Chalk Cliffs. You follow me and do what I say until I get the lay of things."

He wheeled, spurred at a gallop. The shelf land ended, and he swung inland from the river and put his horse up a steep climb. It was less than half a minute to the crest. More river flats lay beyond, and in the distance some cliffs that were white as porcelain by moonlight. They were the limestone formation known as the Chalk Cliffs.

"Steamboat," Big Jim said.

Warren saw the craft a moment later. It was a huge, dark hulk which seemed to have run itself aground on the mudbanks at the far side of the stream, perhaps a mile and a quarter away.

The hammer of guns was suddenly close. Here and there a flash and streak of burning powder cut the darkness from timber shadow along shore. No apparent plan or order, no telling who was the attacked and who the attacker. Apparently no one was shooting at the steamboat. It lay quietly, with black smoke climbing from its twin chimneys.

Cap paused only momentarily at the crest, then he rode on across a quarter mile on flat ground, drawing up in the black-shadowed bottom of a coulée that ran down to the river.

"Here, dammit, you wait. I'll go yonder for a look." Cap started on by himself, then he glanced around and tried to pick Warren from the darkness. "Pecos?"

Warren rode with him up a steep, crumbling bank. A stray bullet whipped close and rattled as it cut through the summer-dry chokeberry twigs. A second bullet cuffed dirt and hummed away.

Sound of shooting did something to Warren, lifting the sense of depression that had settled on him through a series of do-nothing days. He laughed, and Cap, hearing him, said: "I'm damn' glad this pleases somebody."

He sat with his lips compressed, eyes rapidly knifing around the flats. "That's Talbott's Sharps." He was referring to one of the guns. "They got 'em pinned down, all right."

The Barbours had stretched a boom of anchored logs to block the river where sandbars thrust the channel close to shore. Ordinarily the pilot would send a skiff ahead to remove the obstruction, but a few men placed on shore would make their mission impossible. However, the boat had been warned, and an attack had come from the hills, pinning Barbour and his men against the river.

"Damn him," Coyne muttered. "Dermott's been waitin' for this."

They watched for half a minute, spotting the position of guns. It was a guess that Dermott had a force of sixty-five or seventy. There were no such numbers available in Miles, so it was probable he'd brought them upriver from Bismarck where hundreds lay out of work after the suspension of building on the N.P.

A new force of men was moving up along the opposite bank, and gunfire from that third direction would obviously make the ranchers' position untenable.

"Seen enough?" Cap asked and, without waiting for an answer, sent his pony crashing brush to the coulée bottom. Hernandez was there, and the others rode in sight a few seconds later.

"We'll take it up that side," Cap said. "Barbour and his boys seem to be pinned along that ten-foot bank upstream from the coulée mouth. Must be their horses are hid in the box elder grove. If we cut loose from behind, Hoss can make a run for it. Only be careful who you shoot at, and wait till I fire the first shot."

Hernandez was crouched in waist-high buckbrush, peering across the shelf land when Warren and Mary Coyne came up beside him.

Warren said: "Pick out one man. And Cap didn't mean Zenis Barbour."

An instant later Cap Coyne shouted—"Hi-ya!"—and cut with his .44. The volley was sudden, and for a few seconds Dermott's men apparently did not realize the attack was centered on them. Then, when they did, most of them thought it was a mistake.

A man bellowed: "It's us, damn ye!"

He was visible for an instant, seventy-five paces across the flats. Warren fired, and the .44 slug made him fling himself aside. He lay on the ground and sent a return bullet that whipped the air by Warren's cheek.

Warren was on one knee, a Colt in each hand. Guns ripped from both sides. It was a baffling hell of fire, and it seemed to delight him. A bullet cuffed the earth and showered him with hard bits of clay. He aimed back at the flash and heard the responding thud of lead, the grunt of a man who was hit.

Feel of the guns, the rock and smash of their explosions, had an effect like alcohol on his system. He fired again, sending lead ripping into another nest of the attackers, and lifted his voice in a rebel yell.

A bullet tore past, so close it still held a sting of burning powder in its trail. Warren knew they'd spotted him. He pitched to one shoulder, rolled, came to a crouch, and both guns ripped again.

Two slugs coming close showered him with sagebrush twigs. He'd seen explosions less than thirty strides away with flame, brownish-red, through billows of drifting powder smoke. Warren fired at the flash, fired again, and heard the hammers fall on empty cylinders.

No telling whether one of the slugs had taken hold in blind shooting like that. He bent down and poked out the smoking cartridge cases, thrust in fresh ones. It gave him time to look around. Hernandez was no longer near him. A second later he saw the man, crawling from sagebrush to sagebrush, evidently headed for a slight bulge of ground that, during some long-past, high-water period, had become heaped with drift logs.

"Come back, you damned greaser!" Warren hissed. "Our own boys will be sniping you."

Warren had reloaded. He moved a short distance, following Hernandez. The shooting had let up momentarily. Dermott's men seemed to have located the attack and withdrawn to form a more compact group.

Cap Coyne was shouting—"Hoss! Hoss!"—over and over. At last an answer came from the beleaguered men by the river. Cap shouted: "Make a run for it. You hear me, Hoss?"

Hoss didn't answer. No telling what he intended to do.

Gunfire rose in fury. Bullets from unknown sources kept scorching across the earth, whipping dirt, fragments of sage. Cap Coyne, from the edge of the brush, was shouting at Hoss Barbour again, but nobody could distinguish a word he said.

Then, suddenly, there was movement and a rumble of hoofs upstream from the box elder grove. Hoss had his men mounted and was making a run for it. One man was in the lead, bent low over the neck of his horse. The rest came in almost a solid mass, climbed a pitch from the river, galloped across the flats. Thirty horses would have been a reasonable guess, so they'd probably left wounded or dead men back there.

Some of the riders fired as they rode, but they were useless bullets, as likely to strike a friend as an enemy. All of Cap Coyne's men were shooting to create a diversion. The noise was baffling. Powder smoke, hanging in the still night air, looked like fog.

One of the riders was hit. He went down. There was a pile up of horses, but they extricated themselves. One of the animals bolted directly toward the enemy guns. He bucked unexpectedly and threw his rider, who fell face first toward the ground. The man seemed to twist over in mid-air. His boot had hung up in the stirrup. He was down, being dragged, his arms tossed over his head. His boot must have come off. He lay huddled on the ground while his horse sunfished away with the stirrups whopping.

The man was stunned. He staggered to his feet. One of Dermott's men was only a dozen paces away. He fired, a deliberate bullet from that deadly range, killing him as he stood stunned and helpless.

Warren aimed and fired. The range was long, and his target uncertain through smoke and darkness, but he sensed, even as he pulled the trigger, that the bullet had gone home. It smashed the man, spinning him halfway around. He took a step, and his legs collapsed, sending him face foremost to earth.

The riders strung out more and more as their horses gained speed across the flats. Two more were hit, but one stayed with his horse, clutching him around the neck. For a few seconds their course had taken them closer to Dermott's men.

Now precious distance was building between them, and bullets made little puffs of dirt at their heels. With three men hit, they'd got out of it better than they'd had a right to.

Warren's guns were empty again. He poked out the cases.

They were beginning to stick from heat and fouling. He reloaded, tried to locate Big Jim and Hernandez.

The Spaniard still moved forward. Warren told him to come back.

"The Flanagans know not how to retreat, *señor!*"

"Come back or I'll bullet-brand you in the rump. We have to get out of here." Warren mentally consigned Hernandez to the devil and turned to look for Mary Coyne.

He called her name without getting an answer. A sickness like nausea ran through him. He should have kept her out of sight beyond the edge of the coulée. He moved back, gun cocked and thumb hooked over the hammer.

"Mary!" he called.

"Here!" she said.

He'd never heard anything as welcome as her voice.

"Hurry."

"I can't." There was something like a tug of effort in her words. He thought she'd been hurt. He stood and hurried toward her voice. She was there in front of him, bent over the body of a man.

Warren saw that it was Yergens, a nester whose place adjoined the Double C on the west.

"You'll have to help me." She was half crying, trying to lift the man's shoulders. "Don't you see I can't do it all by myself?"

Yergens had been struck high up on the chest, and the bullet had traveled all the way through.

"He's dead," Warren said. There was no time to be subtle about it. "You can't help him now. Come along." He grabbed her, shook her back and forth as though awakening her. "Come along!"

She stopped crying suddenly. "All right," she whispered. "I'm sorry."

"This way."

Someone had been bellowing commands, and men on the far side of the coulée seemed to be executing a wheeling movement that was familiar enough to anyone who had fought through the War Between the States.

Cap Coyne, deep in brush up the coulée, was calling his daughter's name.

"I'm all right!" she shouted back. "Run for it!"

A man fired at the sound of her voice.

"Nice people, these Yankees," Warren said through his teeth. "Is this the way they always treat women up here?"

Shooting had almost stopped. A lull, then an intense exchange about a hundred and fifty yards up the coulée. And after ten seconds that leveled off.

The horses should be deep in brush at the coulée bottom, forty or fifty paces farther along. Big Jim led the way, with Mary after him, and then Warren. A bank opened before them. There was soft earth and waist-deep brush, and black shadow at the bottom.

"Jarvis!" The unfamiliar voice was close ahead in the dark. Alarm tightened the voice as he repeated: "Jarvis!"

The man lunged up and started back when he saw the huge shadow of Jim Swing beside him. There was a rifle in his hands. He started to bring it around, but Jim seized the rifle with one hand, his collar with the other. The man writhed, helpless in Jim's tremendous grasp. He tried to scream for help, but the sound was pinched off in his throat. Then, with a quickness unsuspected in one of his bulk, Jim shifted his hold, lifted the man, and slammed him belly down across his bent knee. He let the man fall, writhing and helpless on the ground.

"Come along!" Warren said.

There was movement from the other coulée bank. A glow of gun shine. Warren was half turned. He spun and started to

draw. Explosion and flame came from an unexpected direction, and the bullet smashed the man back, with his gun firing
wildly and without any aim into the night.

The horses, spooky from gunfire, were tied a couple dozen
steps farther on. Six of them. It was their first hint that
someone besides Yergens had been killed. They mounted
and commenced picking their way up the coulée.

It branched, and there was a wide area of brush. For a
quarter minute there had been no shooting. Little sounds
commenced being audible—the clatter of pebbles underfoot,
an occasional snap of dry brush, the drumming sound as a
prairie chicken was frightened into flight.

So they covered a hundred yards, and another hundred.
The trees played out, leaving only scattered rose thorn and
sage. They rode up the side, and across open ground to the
clay hills without drawing a shot.

# X

## "GUN DOWN"

It was graying off toward dawn when they struck Hoss Barbour's trail and followed it across the Mandan Springs area to the old Broken Arrow place. Horses had been turned loose in the corrals, and a light burned in the log house, but there was no sentry posted.

"Dermott's boys could still ride here and kill the bunch," Cap Coyne muttered, swinging to the ground.

He was too old for hard riding. It took him a while to limp a semblance of usefulness back in his legs. He told Tab Mayberry to put his horse away and limped across the ranch yard. No one had lived at the Broken Arrow for more than a year, and cheat grass was growing along the path that led to the cabin door. A man saw him and sprang out with a rifle in his hands while Cap cursed him.

"Sure," Cap said, "I'm Dermott in person. I got Wally and Tom Carson with me. Left Eldad Stark back yonder in the corral."

Hoss Barbour limped to the door and peered out. He'd been wounded in the left thigh, and most of his pants leg had been cut away. "Lay off'n him, Cap," he growled.

Cap walked inside. Warren followed him, then Jim Swing, Hernandez Flanagan, and the rest, as many as could get inside the door.

The cabin was all one big room. Men filled it. Cap said: "Well, most of you made it. A damn' sight more'n deserved to make it."

Cap stood and looked around the room, dimly revealed in the flame of a bacon-grease lamp. Most of the men were hunkered around the wall, looking tired and dusty. A couple were wounded, lying on saddle blankets in the bunks. One of them was Tom Barbour, the other a cowboy called Buck Boland.

"Jib got killed," Hoss called.

Zenis Barbour had been standing behind the table, holding a tin cup over the lamp flame, trying to make its contents boil. He banged it down and said: "You hear him say Jib got killed?"

"Yes. I'm sorry about it," Cap said.

"You was a long time in saying so."

Eben Smith said: "We had enough fights for one night."

Zenis gestured with his left hand, meaning for him to keep still. He wove around the table with men giving him room. Some of those along the wall sensed trouble and started to get to their feet. Hoss generally stopped Zenis, but this time he didn't say a word.

"Yes, my brother got killed. They was down there, ready for us. They knew what was up. Dermott's got a man planted here. A spy." He wasn't talking to Cap Coyne now. His eyes had traveled beyond Cap and were resting on Warren. And after him on Hernandez. "You hear that? A spy!"

Warren spoke in a voice that sounded dry and tired: "You mean it's me, or Flanagan, don't you? You've forgotten one thing. You planned that attack yonder without letting us know a thing about it, Zenis."

"You got ways of finding things out."

"You forgot something else. You'd all be wolf bait by this time if Cap and the rest of us hadn't saved your hides." He laughed without making it sound pleasant. "I did it because I like you, Zenis. You're such a nice fellow to have around."

"I ain't takin' your lip any more'n Hoss is."

"Zenis, you been looking for it a long time." Warren's voice sounded extremely quiet, and extremely deadly, and there was a stampede of men out of the way.

"Not here, boys," somebody cried.

Cap Coyne turned, grabbed Warren, wrestled him toward the wall. Warren twisted part way free. Zenis Barbour was all alone between the table and the wall. His hand came up, weighted by his .44 Colt. Coyne glimpsed the movement, let go, and hurled himself against the wall.

No one had actually seen Warren draw his right hand revolver, but it was there. It seemed to hesitate, poised and aimed for a fragment of time before it bucked in his hand and lashed flame across the ill-lighted room. Zenis was spun halfway around. The gun in his hand exploded, driving splinters from the floor in front of his boot toes.

Bullet shock left him rammed between wall and table, propped erect. He went down with one leg folded and the other thrust out, with a spur leaving a line of tiny dots across the floor. The gun was still in his hand, but its barrel was pinned between his right hip and the door.

Warren had moved back the instant he fired, and now his shoulders were flat against the wall, and in that position he was momentarily safe from the other Barbour boys.

"He's not killed," Warren said. "I always like to waste one on your kind."

Hoss lurched to the middle of the room. He stood, reared high, the bullwhip clutched in his right hand, looking gorilla-huge beneath the low ceiling. He stared at Warren a second, at the gun, back at his face.

"You ain't got me turned yella-gutted. I'll cut your damn' head off at your shoulders, gun or no."

He swung the whip up and around. It made a roaring sound through the air. Warren could have killed him. He didn't. He bent aside, and the lash did not reach him. Big Jim Swing had rammed his way forward, caught it with an up-flung arm, ripped back, jerking the stock free of Hoss Barbour's hand.

It took Hoss a second to realize what had taken place. Then he roared his rage and turned on Jim Swing. He didn't try to draw. There was a heavy, three-legged stool beside him. He swept it up and charged. Big Jim let the stool strike his forearm and bound away. His right fist swung up in a short smash that connected with Hoss Barbour's jaw. Hoss didn't even see it coming. It snapped him back at the waist, and Hoss sat down, his jaw sagging, eyes off focus.

Cap Coyne stopped a general battle by leaping to the center of the room and waving men back: "No. Dammit, let's not fight amongst ourselves."

Things finally quieted down. Zenis Barbour was not seriously wounded. The bullet had broken a rib or two near his right armpit, but the big artery that fed his arm was not severed. He let Eben Smith lay him on the table to swab it out.

One of the men brought sagebrush and started a fire in the fireplace. Afterward he packed a little pyramid of coal around it. The coal had come from a pit back of the house where the owners had once dug for well water.

Warren examined a piece of it. It was soft coal, but not the gray stuff, half shale, one often sees cropping out in those badlands.

One of the Texas crowd said: "You strike that stuff all along the Springs. Now if we had it in Dodge City, it'd be worth a million."

Warren tossed it back in the fire. It was true there were uncounted millions in that country waiting for development. Cap Coyne came around and asked him to ride back toward the river and scout Dermott's men. Warren knew he wasn't so much concerned in scouting as in getting him out of the Barbours' way. As things stood, there'd probably be a shoot-out before nightfall.

# XI

## "BEEF AT MILES TOWN"

It was sunup when he led Hernandez and Big Jim away from the Broken Arrow, taking a short-cut trail through the little hills. Half an hour later they looked down on the far-flung flats of Mandan Springs. It was still early, with purplish haze hanging in coulée shadows. Smoke rose from a point half a dozen miles away. It was too big for a cook fire.

Warren said: "That's Eben Smith's place. They burned it. Dermott's men."

They rode down several gentle benches, but there was no need of going closer. They could see all that was left—a few corrals, some charred rectangles of sill logs where the houses had been. Other traces of smoke rose from greater distance.

A gray streak ascended from the direction of Cap Coyne's Double C. The streak grew until it became a huge, black billow. An hour later, topping a bulge of the valley floor, they could see the smoldering remains of ranch house, bunkhouses, sheds. No one was in sight. Horses had been turned from the corrals and scattered.

"There's old Jinks," Jim said, pointing at a big bay. "We better round up our remuda, if we can find 'em."

Warren nodded. He kept on toward the smoking ruins. A man was lying face down about halfway between the creek and what was left of the house. One tuft of his fine grayish hair kept blowing in the morning breeze. It was the cook—Jack Snow. He'd been running, and the bullet had taken him between the shoulders.

"We will keel the man who did that," whispered Hernandez.

"I was thinking the same thing," Warren said softly.

They buried Snow, and Hernandez repeated a prayer in Spanish. Afterward they dug in the ruins of the blacksmith shop and rescued their scorched warbags that had been saved by a cave-in of the thick log walls. Then, after roping fresh horses, they rode on toward Miles.

It took them till mid-afternoon. There was a great deal of beef along the way, trail stock, lean from hard travel. Miles Town presented a different aspect, too. It was spread over twice its former area by reason of several hundred canvas-topped Conestoga wagons, tents, and various lesser shelters that had been tossed up. The streets were so crowded they had trouble finding a hitch rack for their mounts.

Warren stopped a tall cowboy who had just clomped from the Carson Brothers' Store and asked if the N.P. was laying rails, after all. It took the cowboy a moment to realize what he meant.

"You mean our new settlers? You can thank Sitting Bull for 'em."

There'd been stories all spring and summer about Sitting Bull's leaving the agency and fomenting trouble among the Western chiefs. The cowboy went on. "He's war-pathin', and he's got the whole Sioux nation behind him. Mandan, Arikara, Dakota, Cheyenne . . . all of 'em. There's talk about High Eagle and the Blackfeet, too."

Warren went on down the street. All anyone could talk about was Sitting Bull and the Sioux. Custer had sent two of his aides, Baker and Reno, to arbitrate, but Sitting Bull had demanded the expulsion of whites from the Black Hills, an area sacred to his people, as a condition of any settlement.

Already there were an estimated two thousand near the new town of Deadwood, working the gold placers, and the demand was impossible. All that Reno could offer was an uncertain "readjustment" of the Minnesota Treaty lands dispute, and Sitting Bull's answer came in three weeks when he attacked Rockford, a settlement west of Deadwood, and massacred twenty men.

The attacks spread, and now his warriors ranged the entire three hundred miles between the Middle Loup and the Belle Fourche, attacking wagon trains, trail herds, and all but the larger settlements. The Black Hills had been isolated now for almost a month with scarcely a freight wagon getting through the blockade, and a man who recently arrived from Deadwood told about jerked buffalo which sold at two dollars a pound, beans at a dollar, flour at seventy dollars a hundred.

Rumors of new Indian outrages continually swept through Miles, were altered in the telling, and then went the rounds again. Sitting Bull with eight hundred braves was sweeping up the Niobrara; Yellowtail had laid siege to Julesburg; Heavy Runner had attacked Densomore and killed a hundred whites, and men believed it even though not a soul in Miles had ever heard of a town by that name before.

A steady succession of wagons, carts, even travois, lurched into town from the south and southeast, nesters mostly, who had abandoned their miserable holdings along the Belle Fourche, the Cheyenne, and the Little Missouri. But, while everyone talked of Sitting Bull, apparently there'd been no news of the fight at the Chalk Cliffs, although the steamboat that played a part in it was at that moment tied to the Dermott docks. The only news concerning the steamboat was that one of its passengers was Senator Wilton Reeves of Kansas.

A bartender at a saloon called The Drag expressed the

opinion that Reeves would "pretty quick make those damned Union generals wake up," and everyone within sound of his voice agreed, probably the same men who had recently been calling him "Carpetbagger Reeves," and wondering why in the hairy old hell he and his whole Washington gang weren't impeached and tossed into jail for their association with the Credit Mobelier scandal.

After a bath, haircut, and shave, Bill Warren started out to find Dermott. It was growing dark. There was a light in his office, but a black-whiskered man named Jack Bell sat just inside the hall, tilted back in his chair, a sawed-off shotgun across his knees.

"You're goin' no farther, cowboy," Bell said.

"Tell Dermott the Pecos Kid wants to see him," Warren said loudly to Bell.

He said it with enough vigor to be heard through the closed door, and, as he'd expected, Dermott came out.

"Warren!" He walked across with his hand thrust out eagerly, a smile showing on his strong teeth. "You've been gone a long time."

"Get my messages?"

"Certainly. I thought you'd know. After last night." He stepped back after shaking hands, and the smile left his face. His jaw became prominent, eyes narrow. "They slipped away from us. I don't understand it *yet*."

Warren didn't like the way he pronounced the word "yet." He kept watching Dermott's eyes. They weren't the kind that ever showed anything

"I have a visitor," Dermott said, jerking his head at the door. "A rather important visitor."

"Senator Reeves?"

"You knew?"

"I guessed. Maybe you want me to come back."

"No. I think I'd like to have you meet the senator." He smiled a trifle. "We're all in this together, aren't we?"

"The senator, too?"

Dermott paused with his hand on the knob. "Senators are human, just like everybody else." He seemed to make a little grimace of distaste when he added: "In fact, *this* senator is about the *most human* senator who ever went to Washington."

Warren knew what he meant. He walked through the door that Dermott held open for him. Only a dim glow came through the big, double windows that looked out across the roofs of warehouses, and the hanging lamp had been lighted. Two men were seated.

One was Wallace Carson, a pale, tall man of forty whose gray hair and stiff dignity made him seem older, and the other, evidently Senator Reeves, was short, soft-looking, and fifty-five. He was pink and clean-shaven, and, although the crown of his head was bald, he attained a senatorial elegance by allowing the hair to grow along the edges until he could comb it back over his ears.

Warren already knew Carson, and shook hands with him. Then he was introduced to the senator.

"Young man!" was all Senator Reeves said, but the stentorian nature of his voice gave the words a sound of importance.

Dermott said: "Mister Warren is one of our associates."

"A cattleman, I dare say," Reeves said in his rich baritone.

"Yes, seh," Warren answered in his soft Texas way.

"Tell me, how are you cattlemen progressing against those nester brigands out at Mandan Springs?" the senator asked. "A disgrace, sir, the thing that is happening to our Public Domain. These persons who insinuate themselves on another's property and defy them with force of arms! Yes, and even grow bolder. Attack the very steamboat that carries a member of the Congress of the United States! I'll have the

Army on these men. I'll not tolerate it, do you understand? We have troops, though sometimes a person would doubt it. I'll demand protection from Colonel Ludloe. I'll demand that he drive those brigands into the river. And if he hasn't men enough, then by the gods I'll send a telegram to General Custer for reinforcements."

"You'll do no such thing," Dermott said. "I want no more men at Fort Keogh than there are now. When the colonel comes, I'd like to have as little importance as possible placed in that affair last night. The Army never insinuated itself into one of these matters yet without interfering with legitimate enterprise."

Warren knew that whatever kept Dermott interested in Mandan Springs lacked something of legitimate enterprise—otherwise he'd not hesitate to use the Army. There was something Dermott didn't want finding its way into the Army records.

Colonel Ludloe arrived about three drinks later. He was a small, erect man of forty-five, possessing the lean reserve that is typical of so many who have spent their lives in the profession of command. He shook hands with Reeves, whom he'd met before, and then with Warren. He gave Warren a sharp scrutiny.

"You were Colonel Warren, serving under Price in Missouri?"

"That was my brother. He was killed. I was Major Warren under Johnston."

"Sorry . . . Major."

"Just the Pecos Kid," Warren said softly. "I'm afraid I didn't earn any such rank from a professional Army man's viewpoint. They weren't sifting their officers so carefully when I was made a major in 'Sixty-Four."

"If you were Colonel Warren's brother, I dare say you

measured up all right. He was a fine soldier. Sorry, I'd never heard he was killed." He turned then to Senator Reeves. There was no deference in his manner, rather a meticulous courtesy. "Senator, I believe you were on the *Princess Jo* last night. I have learned there was some sort of an attack made on it."

Reeves spread his fat fingers deprecatingly. "These rumors! What haven't I heard since I arrived here? Sioux in solid phalanx all the way from Miles to Leavenworth. And yet we know that Sitting Bull could raise no more than a thousand warriors. Now a bit of nonsensical shooting from a half-dozen firebrands who have a pique against the big interests, and immediately this town of yours magnifies it to a scale of piracy unknown since the days of Elizabeth. I'm surprised at a hard-headed old Army man like you giving any credence to it."

Reeves carried it off excellently, and yet there was a look in Ludloe's eyes that indicated something short of conviction. "What was the cause of the shooting?" he asked Dermott.

"Everybody shoots at me," Dermott said. "During last year I lost a total of a hundred and thirteen freight wagons and almost five hundred head of stock to an assortment of cut-throats, white and red, here and there between Fort Benton and Cheyenne, and I can't recall any previous demonstration of concern on the part of the Army."

"My forces are spread thin even when I try to cover my own parade ground, Dermott." Ludloe looked back to the senator. "For a long time we've been trying to get reinforcements for Fort Keogh. Lord knows, sitting here in the midst of Sioux territory, we need them worse than they do to the east of the Mississippi."

Carpetbagger Reeves cleared his throat and assured Ludloe he would give the matter his scrutiny. "You must understand General Custer's difficulty, sir. I was dining with him at the cantonment in Fort Leavenworth only three weeks ago. He told me he'd had more than two hundred desertions since the discovery of gold in the Black Hills."

"I understand Custer's difficulty, but why should the Army have more men stationed in Illinois than in Montana Territory?"

"I will give the matter my scrutiny, and I shall *insist* on the West receiving its just apportionment of the troops."

Colonel Ludloe thanked him, withdrew, and closed the door behind him. His absence seemed to leave the senator a little less jittery. He poured another drink.

"I fail to see your position, Dermott," Reeves said. "If you want these nesters driven off the railroad sections, why not let me use pressure to bring Fort Keogh up to strength? Let the Army do the job."

"I said I wanted the Army kept out of it," Dermott said. "I don't care to give Ludloe the chance of poking into my affairs."

"Sir, you'll have a hard time preventing the reinforcement of Keogh if this Indian business grows worse."

"I won't prevent it. *You'll* prevent it," Dermott said.

"Damn it, I have to think of my reputation."

"Beginning when?"

"The people, sir." Senator Reeves held up one finger. "I am governed by their opinions. No matter what you think, no senator, no matter how firmly established. . . ."

"Can you keep Custer from reinforcing Keogh for two more weeks?" Dermott asked.

"Not if Sitting Bull attacks along the Belle Fourche," the senator mused.

"Then it's up to Sitting Bull, and not you," the steamboat owner said.

"I'm afraid that's the situation." The senator nodded.

"It was a mistake for me to bring you here," Dermott snapped. "Very well, we'll have to clean up the situation before then." Dermott did some cursing. "We should have finished it last night. Those limping fools should have wiped them out when they had them cornered along the river. Do you know how many men I brought down from Bismarck for that job?" he asked Warren. "One hundred and twenty-six! It'll cost me better than ten thousand dollars. I'll pick fifty from the lot and send the *Princess Jo* back with the rest in the morning. There aren't one in four of those railroad riffraff who can handle a gun, and not one in ten knows enough to hold his tongue. If I could only have waited for my own freight crews to get in. There are some fighting men for you."

Warren said: "Mandan Springs will turn out to be the most expensive ranching land in the West."

"But bottomed by gold, sir," the senator said. "Black gold."

Dermott turned on him with one of his sharp, exasperated movements. "And not one senator in ten knows enough to hold his tongue, either!"

There was no more said concerning black gold. Dermott kept pacing the room. He usually reached his decisions rapidly, and his failure to come to one now seemed to upset him. At last he said: "Sitting Bull is almost sure to attack toward the Belle Fourche. Maybe he'll try to burn Miles. That medicine man will try anything. If he does, there'll be five hundred soldiers tramping down the street as soon as a steamboat can haul them. We have to settle this business at Mandan or have it settled for us. Warren, they still trust you. Can you bring their leaders in here for some kind of compromise?"

"What are you going to offer?"

"I'll pay railroad prices for their cattle. Every hoof. The

rest we'll turn over to the senator's arbitration. You can go out there tomorrow morning. As a symbol of good faith, I'll send three thousand in gold as a down payment. I dare say that's more money than they've seen since they left Texas."

# XII

# "POWWOW"

Warren went outside. Big Jim was seated on the loading platform, talking to a couple of freighters. He asked about Hernandez, and a moment later saw the Spanish-Irishman coming from across the street. He'd been atop one of the warehouse roofs, looking into Dermott's window.

"I thought perhaps they would keel you," Hernandez said cheerfully. "I was never one to miss watching a man get keeled, *señor*." Hernandez already smelled of brandy, but he'd done a better than average job of keeping himself sober. "It is that I am like a *peon* without money," he added bitterly, when Warren looked as if he would congratulate him. "You see me, *señor,* broke and bankrupt, with my pockets empty. I have been watching from the roof to see if that king of the steamboats would give you money, for I would have my share."

"I didn't get a two-bit piece from him."

"Are you then a fool that . . . ?"

"We'll collect. With interest. This is one town we're not going to ride away from broke."

Warren had one drink with Hernandez and Big Jim at the Round Tent, then he walked to the docks where he hired a rowboat to take him across the river to Fort Keogh. He could tell at first glance that the place was ridiculously undermanned. Only one of the barracks buildings was inhabited. A Negro private led him through the gate and escorted him

94

across the parade ground to Colonel Ludloe's house.

Ludloe seemed glad to see him. An orderly was just serving him coffee. He asked for an extra cup and proceeded to lace both with brandy.

"Why should Roger Dermott oppose the reinforcing of Fort Keogh?" Warren asked.

"Dermott is like a busy blacksmith. He has many hot irons, and he has to handle some of them fast to keep from getting burned. I don't engage in speculations that don't involve the military." The coffee was too hot to drink, but Ludloe sat and held the cup close to his nostrils, breathing the brandy fumes. "It seems to me that *I* am the one who should have asked *you* that question."

"I'm only one of his hot irons."

"Those Mandan Springs ranchers attacked the *Princess Jo* last night, didn't they?" Ludloe mused.

"And Dermott was ready for them."

"He was afraid I'd horn in and get it in an Army report. He was wrong. The Army is here for one purpose, and that's to keep the Indians under control."

"But you could get reinforcements, if you had to," Warren said.

"I could. The Western Department needs more troops . . . that's what I was talking about to the senator. Custer will send more troops here if he decides Sitting Bull's main attack is aimed at Miles and the valley of the Yellowstone rather than at Deadwood, or Fort Pierre, or at the Union Pacific railroad. He has just so many men, and he'll have to deploy them the best he can."

"When will you know about the Sioux?"

"Tonight. Next week. Next month. No man can tell what an Indian will do. I have my scouts out, of course. Four of them are Poncas, so I don't know if they can be trusted. I'd rather have Crees to scout the Sioux. They hate them worse."

Warren finally got around to the real point of his visit and asked what was so valuable about Mandan Springs.

Ludloe drank some of his brandied coffee and repeated what he'd already said about not engaging in speculations that did not involve the military.

"I have an idea this can damn' well involve the military before it's finished," Warren said. "Do you know anything about coal deposits over there?"

"Any man can see coal cropping out in the badlands all the way through Dakota and Montana. I doubt that much of it will be valuable in our lifetime." He stood up and walked to a large map of the area. "By the way, the Geodetic Survey made some mention of coal strata in its report on that country near the Springs. Horizontal strata, pretty shallow."

"Where could I see their report?"

"In Washington. It was the *Geodetic* . . . not the geologic . . . Survey. I doubt they'd much more than mention it."

"That's railroad land. They'd own all the minerals, wouldn't they?"

"If it's railroad land, they'd own it on alternate sections. The N.P. land isn't solid, you know. It's like a checkerboard."

"*If* they owned it?"

"Why, yes. If they own it."

"How could I find out *if* they own it?" Warren asked.

"Certainly not from me. But there's a Land Office in town . . . a man by the name of Wallace Gates keeps it open between drinks. The plats should be in his office."

Warren finished his drink, picked up his hat, and excused himself. Ludloe followed him outside. "Just who are you working for?" he asked.

"Why, lately, I've decided to start working for a man by

the name of Jim Swing. I need a considerable sum of money to keep him out of the sheep business." Warren grinned, and strolled off.

The Land Office was a narrow, low shanty with a bent-board roof. No light. Gates, who claimed the title of U.S. commissioner, proved to be a tall, seedy, would-be lawyer of fifty, and, as Ludloe suggested, he was out for a drink.

"Closed at six, government regulation," he protested, but Warren forced him through the swinging doors of the Long-horn Bar and down the sidewalks to his office. There Gates got the door unlocked and groped inside, falling over obstructions and finally lighting the lamp. The place was heaped with books, documents, and dirty dishes on table, chairs, the floor.

"What can I do for you, sir?" he asked, getting himself seated beside a high secretary desk.

"I want to see the government survey maps."

"What particular district?"

"Mandan Springs."

Gates had already started to reach for some rolled-up maps. His hand stopped, and his eyes narrowed. The words had jolted him quite sober. "They are not available."

"The Army has assured me that they were."

"You go tell the Army. . . ."

Warren took a step forward, seized Gates by the collar, and rammed him back in the chair. He tried to rise, but he was helpless against Warren's strength.

"Give me those maps!"

Gates shook his head back and forth and tried to answer, but the air was pinched from his vocal chords. Warren let up a little.

"They're . . . not here," Gates wheezed.

"Where are they?"

"In Bismarck. Railroad business. . . ."

"You're lying." His fingers tightened again. "You're lying."

Gates's face was turning dark. Little drops of spittle showed at the corners of his mouth. His lips formed the words: "Yes."

Warren held him for a while anyway. "Where are they?"

"I loaned them. To . . . Dermott."

"When?"

"I forget. Damn it, I don't remember little things. Maybe . . . two months ago . . . last spring."

Warren let him go. Gates got to his feet, leaned against the wall. He started forward, tripped, and fell headlong across the floor. Warren watched him crawl to his knees, grope for a chair, pull himself to its seat.

"Just forget I came here," Warren said.

Gates nodded his head. He still breathed with a scraping sound. His eyeballs were sharp, distended. "Sure. I don't ever want to remember you."

Warren left him there. He walked up the street and looked inside the Round Tent. Hernandez was at his old place by the roulette wheel, but there weren't a great many chips in front of him.

The orchestra was playing, and the theater was jammed with dancing couples. Most of the men were refugees from Sioux country to the southeast, but they all seemed to have money to spend on the short-skirted dance-hall girls.

Music stopped and the girls steered their partners to tables and the bar to collect percentage brass for the "house drink," and during the intermission a tenor on stage launched forth on "A Handful of Earth from Dear Old Mother's Grave." For some reason never fully explained, a man is always more generous in tears than in laughter.

A familiar figure was seated at a table on the balcony. It was Lona Pearl. Warren moved back to the sidewalk and walked to the steamboat docks.

The boilers of the *Princess Jo* breathed softly under a low head of steam, and somewhere a Negro crewman was singing.

**All night down in the engine deck
I shovel in de coal.
I'd rather be a gamblin' man
And wear de ring o' gol'. . . .**

There was no light in Dermott's office, but the windows had been left open. Warren walked to the river side of the building. The eaves were low, and it was no great task getting to the roof. From there he could see that the second story was merely a shack-like addition set atop the warehouse. He climbed to the second roof, crouched for a while, watching for movement below, then lowered himself, clinging to the fancy molding along the front, until his feet touched the window sill. A few seconds later he was inside.

He stood up in the inner darkness. The office seemed close and hot. He scratched a match, opened the drawers of Dermott's desk, moved on to some cases along the wall. Nothing that looked like maps. He finally found the map he was looking for inside a cluttered little storeroom.

There, with a lamp heating the close confines of the room, he spread the map on the floor and examined it. It took him a while to orient himself, then he saw that the railroad sections barely touched Mandan Springs. Ludloe's hint had been correct. Neither the railroad nor Dermott owned the land.

Things started to clear up in his mind. He could see the situation that had confronted Dermott. There was coal across those broad flats—shallow layers of coal. It was worthless as dirt at the present time, but, when the railroad came, it could be worked by means of spur lines and steamshovels at a fraction of the cost entailed in underground methods. The resulting produce could be shipped directly back to the new milling and manufacturing center at Minneapolis or on to Butte, where vast mineral deposits had been unearthed.

Dermott would have purchased the area, but he was prevented by land policy and the Homestead Act. He'd have laid claim to it under the Non-Metallic Minerals Act, but squatters occupied the ground, and squatter sovereignty was not a thing to be laughed at. So he had decided to bluff. He knew that no man could follow the infrequent survey marks laid through that limitless country. He knew that no one, not even the moguls of the Northern Pacific themselves, quite knew where their vast land holdings were located. So he had bought options on railroad land which he claimed to cover Mandan Springs.

Warren put everything back as he'd found it, climbed from the window, dropped to the ground. There was no sign that anyone had seen him.

# XIII

## "CONFAB"

He'd been a long time without sleep, so it was mid-morning before he got around to Dermott's office and picked up the three thousand in gold. At noon he headed out of town by himself, and that evening he reached the Broken Arrow.

Warren clomped inside and strewed gold pieces across the kitchen table.

"There's the down payment," he said as men gathered around, staring at the first real money they'd seen in months.

"Down payment on what?" Hoss Barbour asked.

"On your cattle. Dermott claims he's willing to buy every hoof at railroad prices. Maybe he'll do it. He wants to meet with you in town. Senator Reeves will be there to arbitrate. He doesn't know it yet, but Colonel Ludloe will be there, too."

"You think there's a chance of us getting a fair show for *that* damn' Yankee?" Hoss asked.

"*Ludloe* is honest. And I have a little surprise that'll knock Dermott right out of his chair," Warren added.

He let them argue it out among themselves, but even Zenis Barbour, wounded, with his arm in a sling, had his natural bitterness tempered by feel of the heavy gold coin. In the end, there was not a single dissenting vote against riding in for the meeting.

A committee was chosen—Zenis and Hoss Barbour, Cap Coyne, Eben Smith, and seven more. Mary Coyne, as usual, went with her father. They arrived in Miles shortly after nightfall.

No one took any special notice of them as they rode up the street, but there were lanterns burning along the front of Dermott's warehouse. If a man looked closely, he could catch movement and flashes of gun shine here and there in the shadows, so Warren knew that they had been expected. He swung down and jingled his spurs across the dusty yard. Big Jim came to meet him.

"Dermott isn't laying a deadfall, is he?" Warren asked.

"I doubt it. Not with seven men, and that's all he's got posted." Jim looked around at the Barbours and grinned. "By damn', I'd want a detail of cavalry if I went for them ornery Barbour boys."

Jim got Warren aside and went on in a lower voice. "There's something damn' strange going on here, Kid. Couple trappers rode in yesterday noon and said the Sioux burned 'em out on Willow Creek. That's between here and the Belle Fourche. Fifty-five men under Calf Robe. They laid out in the bushes and counted 'em. Same day a cowboy named Mader outrun forty Sioux on the upper Lodgepole. You remember that Clawhammer outfit that was driving to the Sweetwater under Dad Slater? He rode with 'em. Anyhow, Mader's no damn' Missouri punkin-roller that sees Sioux behind every sagebrush. It adds up that Sitting Bull is aimed right straight at the Yellowstone."

"Did you see Colonel Ludloe?"

"Saw him this afternoon. He said he'd have to get word on it from his own scouts. Couldn't believe all these stories."

"That's true, Jim," Warren said. "If the Army believed all the stories that hit this town, they'd have troops scattered from Dodge to Fort Benton."

"Hold on! That ain't the all of it. Now comes the peculiar

part. You know Hernandez . . . ?"

"Hernandez Pedro Gonzales y Fuente Jesús María Flanagan? You mean Butch?"

"This is no time to joke, Kid. What I was going to say was that Hernandez now and then gets snooted up on high wine and acts like he was locoed, but he ain't. He's only half crazy. The Irish half. That Mex' half of him stays sharp and suspicious as the blade of that Bowie he carries. Last night Lona Pearl got him to singing songs in her apartment, and next asking about you and little Mary. To make the story short, Butch staggered through the wrong door on purpose and guess what he found. A half-breed Ponca asleep on Johnny Malette's couch with an empty bottle of Hennessey in his hand. Doesn't that seem sort of funny to you, Kid?"

"Did you tell Ludloe?" Warren asked.

"I ain't had a chance."

"Ride over there. Tell him to come up to Dermott's office. Tell him I said it was important. And tell him about the half-breed, too."

Dermott wasn't in his office. They ate and returned, a heavily armed, suspicious group. This time Dermott was waiting on the loading platform.

"Glad to see you boys," he said, with every appearance of sincerity.

Hoss Barbour was in the lead. He chawed for a while and looked at Dermott with narrow-eyed suspicion.

"You don't need to act any friendlier than you feel. I want you to know that I hate your Yankee guts, and I'm willing to fight you down to the last cartridge." Then he tempered it by adding: "If that's the way you want it."

"That's not the way I want it. I want to start out from here, and to hell with what's past. This is no time to be fighting with the Sioux swarming around Deadwood."

"You're peaceful?"

"I'm peaceful," Dermott said.

"Then why you got them lads stationed by the river?"

"For the same reason you have Colts on your hips and Winchesters across your arms. You lighten that cargo of Hartford metal, and I'll send my boys uptown for a drink."

"Let 'em go thirsty," Hoss muttered. "I ain't unbucklin' my guns."

They climbed to the office, and Dermott sent one of his warehousemen out for more chairs. It took a while. The ranchers ranged the wall, looking big, and rough, and truculent. Finally everyone was seated.

Dermott tapped at the door of an adjoining sitting room and said: "Would you care to come out now, Senator?"

Senator Reeves made his entrance, carrying a legal volume and a thick folder of documents. He placed these things carefully on the edge of the desk and spoke: "Gentlemen! May I say I have already conducted an independent investigation in the matter that brings us together, and I see no reason why a settlement cannot be made that would be advantageous to both sides." He cleared his throat and looked at Hoss Barbour. "Most advantageous."

Hoss was not awed. He chewed and spurted a stream of tobacco juice across the floor.

"A carpetbagger if I ever seen one."

Dermott said: "Oh, hell, Hoss, a senator has to use big words or else folks will find out he's human."

Dermott had lived a rough life, associating with aristocrats and buffalo hunters, spending one summer in fine hotels, the next sleeping on the ground in Indian country, and he'd developed a way of getting along with people, of speaking their language. One could see his personality working now. These ranchers were commencing to like him in spite of themselves.

Dermott called—"Joseph."—but nobody came. He said something about "that damn' boy," and got up to pull the cork from a bottle of whiskey himself. He didn't bother with glasses. He wiped the neck with his coat sleeve and started it on its rounds by handing it to Hoss.

It got back to him with a couple ounces left. He tilted it up, killed it, and threw it out the open window. By that time Joseph was there. He sent him out for more whiskey. Then he sat back and talked. He had an easy way with him.

He started by admitting that his fight for Mandan Springs had cost him twenty thousand dollars already, and that another twenty thousand was more than the country was worth. He talked for a long time, and it was not the speech of a man who had his opponents against the wall. It was the speech of a man admitting his defeat and resigned to be cheerful about it.

He dipped a pen and wrote the figure **3,000** in big letters across the top of a sheet of paper, and beneath it: **First Payment**.

"I'll pay gold coin for your cattle," he said. "At railhead prices. Do you hear that, Senator? Gold at railhead prices. See that I'm held to it."

"Indeed, sir! There is not a banker west of Saint Louis that would not take those words as a bond."

The whiskey arrived and was passed around. After half an hour, Dermott's real purpose in bringing the ranchers there was still in no way discernible. It was almost as though he were on the level. Only he was too generous. These ranchers were about licked, and they knew it.

It occurred to Warren that Big Jim had plenty of time to get Colonel Ludloe. He rolled a cigarette. He'd almost smoked it when he heard Colonel Ludloe's voice addressing Jack Bell outside.

Dermott recognized the voice and stopped talking. "Come in!" he called without giving Ludloe a chance to knock.

Ludloe stood and gave the men a careful scrutiny. He nodded to Warren, Dermott, the senator.

Dermott said: "Is there something you wanted, Colonel?"

"I was asked to sit in on your conference."

The words jolted Dermott, but he mastered any visible show of surprise. "There must be some mistake."

"I think not," the Pecos Kid said softly. "*I* asked the colonel."

Dermott's jaw jutted more than usual, muscles knotted at its sides, and veins distended at his temples, all showing the fury he was trying to hold in check. "Ridiculous! The colonel has enough trouble of his own. . . ."

"I'd like to sit in, if these men don't mind," Ludloe said, indicating the ranchers.

"Hell, no," said Hoss. "Grab yourself a piece of floor and squat."

"This does not concern the Army," Dermott said.

"Would you let me be the judge of that?" the colonel said.

Ludloe preserved his scrupulous courtesy, and the words were more cutting because of it. He went on, talking to Dermott: "It is my understanding that you have purchased options on certain grant lands of the Northern Pacific Railroad. As one of my duties is to protect such grants from unlawful seizure, would you mind letting me see those options?"

Dermott started to answer, but he couldn't trust himself. He reached for the whiskey bottle, and fury made it shake in his hand. He slammed the bottle back to the table with a force that made some of its contents jump from the open neck and spill across his hairy forearm. Then he said in a tight voice:

"They're in my vault. Downstairs. It will require some delay and. . . ."

"Would you mind sending for them?"

"Joseph!" Dermott shouted savagely. He sat, still clutching the whiskey bottle, waiting for the Negro boy to come.

# XIV

## "HOT BOX"

Big Jim Swing returned from Fort Keogh and seated himself on the loading platform of Dermott's warehouse. Two Negroes were unloading a cargo of buffalo pelts from a jerkline freight outfit that had just rolled in from the southwest. Overhead, from the open window of Dermott's office, he could hear the steady sound of voices. He smoked his way through a cigarette.

A coyote had howled. It was such an ordinary sound he didn't think of its nearness. A violin was playing the "Blue Velvet Polka" up the street, and he was enjoying its rhythm. It suddenly occurred to him how strange it was that a coyote should be howling there, in the midst of the settlement.

The sound came again. He crushed out his cigarette and walked around the freight wagons. He had a careless way about him that tended to minimize his frame and muscle which were on the scale of a Percheron horse. He watched the rambling, shed-roofed buildings across the way. A twenty-foot passage between them lay deep in night shadow. He groped along it, heard movement, stopped. Hernandez Flanagan's voice came from above.

"*Señor,* if any women come looking for their Hernandez, you may tell them I have a good place to watch for stars." He was lying on the roof, head thrust over the edge, grinning down on him.

"Damn it all, Butch, this ain't any time for jokes," said Big Jim.

"To the Spaniard, love is not a joke. Love is the air he breathes, the wine he drinks. But tonight, while I watched the stars, I saw many stars, I saw many horsemen leaving this town. Perhaps *Señor* Dermott only keeps those men in his office so he can attack the others at the Broken Arrow. In my country, *señor,* this is an old military maneuver known as the 'Keek With the Pants Down.' It would perhaps be wise to tell the Kid what strategy their General Yellow-Guts Dermott has planned for them."

Big Jim walked back, trying to appear casual about it, but his strides were half again as long as usual. The freight wagons were still being unloaded. He circled them, walked along the platform, climbed the outside stairs.

He stopped abruptly just inside the door. Jack Bell had rammed a sawed-off shotgun against his stomach.

"Where you been, cowboy?"

"That's none of your damn' business."

"Don't get mouthy. Ever see a man get hit by an ounce of buck? It turns him inside out like an old feather tick. I asked where you been."

Big Jim could think of no good answer. He moved aside, hoping to get away, but the gun muzzle followed him. He found himself against the wall. His eyes kept moving to the gun and back to Bell's whiskered face. Bell rammed the muzzle, and Big Jim retreated. There was a door at the far end of the hall, and a dark room beyond.

"Right through the door, cowboy," Bell said.

He noticed at the same instant that the shotgun was angled away from his abdomen. He started to turn, but something hit him. For a moment he seemed suspended while the world spun and an intense ringing rose in his ears.

Big Jim was down on hands and knees. He tried to lunge and grapple, but his arms and legs were heavy as though his veins flowed liquid lead. He was struck again, and again, each successive blow driving him deeper into a whirlpool of darkness. Finally he passed out cold.

Dermott had time to get control of himself, while waiting for his bookkeeper to bring the railroad land options. He passed the bottle around and made some easy talk, but Warren knew that anger had settled cold and hard inside him. The options proved to be conditional bills of sale, devised to become effective with the final payments three, four, and five years in the future. Naturally he never intended to redeem them after the Mandan area once came into his hands.

Ludloe read through a couple of them.

"Satisfied?" Dermott asked.

Warren spoke: "Those aren't options on any land lying inside the limits of Mandan Springs."

Dermott must have been ready for something like that. He showed no surprise, no longer any visible sign of anger. He laughed, an easy, modulated sound. He seemed to be genuinely amused.

"Then I've been cheated. Just where are they, if not in Mandan Springs?"

"Down in the badlands between Cap Coyne's Double C and the river," Warren said.

"No. I'm not that great a fool. They cover every alternate square mile of land from the old Block M cabin to within ten miles of Powder River."

The senator was leafing through the papers.

"Sir, your allegation is preposterous," he said to Warren. "These options are obviously legal instruments covering the land specified. See, in each one the words 'Mandan Springs Quadrangle' is specifically. . . ."

"Keep your yawp closed, you fat-gutted carpetbagger!"

Hoss Barbour brayed. "That's the Pecos Kid you're talkin' to. He used to be an officer in the Army of the Confed'racy! He understands them things. What in hell do you know about surveyin'? How do you know about the Springs? You never been there."

"Sir, you will not address me in that manner."

"Keep still or I'll whop your teeth down your throat."

Hoss might have tried it, but Cap Coyne got hold of one arm and Colonel Ludloe was facing him. Dermott, meanwhile, moved a few things on his desk and kept smiling.

"Damn' Yankee," Hoss wheezed, sitting down.

"Hoss is right," Dermott said. "The words 'Mandan Springs Quadrangle' could mean lots of things besides the Mandan Springs *area*. The Quadrangle covers many miles. It means a folio of the atlas. But those options are still correct. They were O Ked by the chief surveyor when he was in Bismarck."

He sounded so reasonable that the ranchers believed him in spite of themselves. Ludloe was looking at Warren.

"Well?"

"You want me to show proof? All right. I can produce it. It's right here in this office."

"Thoughtful of me to keep it handy, wasn't it?" Dermott said.

For the first time, suspicion knifed through Warren—suspicion that Dermott had been forewarned. Warren stood up and opened the closet expecting to find that the survey map had disappeared. It hadn't. It was still there, exactly as he'd left it. He carried it out, untied the string, unrolled it on Dermott's desk. He looked down and met Dermott's eyes. They were narrow and hard as blue-gray flint. His lips were pulled tightly, showing his strong teeth. He was still smiling.

Led by Hoss, the ranchers had left their chairs to crowd

around. The senator, who'd had experience in such things, was already comparing the section numbers of options with corresponding squares on the map. The map was not the same. Its township numbering had been changed, and the lightly shaded checkerboard of N.P. land now covered the entire Mandan area.

Warren could feel perspiration crawling along his hairline. Not once, in all their dealings, had Dermott been fooled. "I shouldn't have underestimated you," Warren said.

"Never overestimate a friend or underestimate an enemy. I have followed that principle for some time," Dermott said.

"You have friends?"

"Why, no, I guess not. They're a prohibitive luxury for a man in my position."

Colonel Ludloe finished his inspection of papers and map. He looked at Warren. "Well? What do you have to say?"

"Nothing it would do any good to say."

"I see." He nodded to the ranchers, to the senator, to Dermott. "Excuse me for intruding."

Ludloe went out the door. As he closed it, Warren had a glimpse of the hall. There were others besides Jack Bell there now. Someone was inside Dermott's sitting room, too. Dermott was talking again. He took up several things that had been covered before. He was killing time, probably waiting for Colonel Ludloe to get back across the river. The room was stifling. Finally Eben Smith said: "Damn it, we've had enough talk. You say you'll pay our price for the places you burned. All right, let's settle it now. I was more'n a year putting up the house and sheds on my place. I wouldn't've sold it for five thousand, and that's my inventory you was askin' for. I'll take the money now."

Dermott looked surprised and perhaps a little offended. "We'll have to draw up the papers. The senator will be in town for a week or more, and it should all come under his scrutiny."

"To hell with the senator," Hoss said. "If you want to buy, I'll sell. The Barbour ranch is worth ten thousand dollars."

"I've already offered to take your cattle. . . ."

"It's worth that *without* the cattle."

"It is my place without the cattle," Dermott laughed, pointing to the options. Hoss started to shout back, but Dermott held up his hand for silence. "Hold on. Think it over till tomorrow morning. You've had a long ride and a tough night. Come back tomorrow at ten. If your offer is reasonable, I'll pay."

They got up and filed outside. Warren started with them, but there was a slight creak as the door to Dermott's sitting room swung a few inches farther open. Dark in there, but not too dark to see a dim shine of gun metal, to make out the outline of tall, slouched Eldad Stark. He was aiming the gun quite steadily at Warren's temple.

"Yes, stay," Dermott said softly, keeping away from the line of fire. "I have a few things I'd like to discuss with you."

Cap Coyne started back from the hall when he saw that Warren was not following, but Dermott went to the door, smiling pleasantly, explaining that Warren would naturally want to take up a few of the technical points with Senator Reeves. Cap was still suspicious.

Warren said easily: "Go ahead, Cap. I'll handle things all right."

Dermott closed the door, bolted it. Then he turned and said: "You act confident of yourself."

"I have a way of squeezing through tight places."

"How old are you, Warren? Twenty-eight? That's old for a man with your reputation. Gunmen don't last that long. Most of them don't last till they're twenty-two."

"Whoever told you I was a gunman? I'm an old Rebel soldier in search of my fortune. Sometimes a man turns up and wants to shoot me. I have them buried all the way from here to San Saba."

"Don't reach for that gun on your hip."

"Why, no. I wouldn't do that. Not while Eldad Stark's in there with those sights notched down on my temple. I'd like to walk out of here alive."

Stark, hearing his name, had moved forward. He was standing in the door. He'd lowered the Colt a little and was holding it waist high. His jaw was loose, exposing his buck teeth. He'd always feared Warren, and hated him. His hatred showed now. His thumb rocked the hammer back. He held the trigger depressed.

Senator Reeves was staring at the gun. His eyes were like those of a man who wakes up and finds a coiled rattler beside his bed. Color had drained from his face, leaving it biliously yellow. He tried to speak, but only a dry hiss came from his throat. At last he said: "That gun. Make him put that gun away."

"Why?" Dermott asked.

"He'll kill Warren."

"Why, sure. What did you think he was going to do? What else is there to do with a traitor than kill him?" Dermott asked.

"No. Good God, Dermott. Not that. Why, I'm here. I can't associate with . . . murder."

Dermott laughed. He walked around the desk, approached Warren so as not to place himself in the line of fire, and plucked the Kid's gun from its holster. He dropped it in the top drawer of his desk. He'd let his own coat come open. He was carrying a Smith & Wesson rimfire .32, a custom-made gun with ivory stocks and engraved silver surfaces.

Aside from the fancy work, it was the same gun Mary Coyne carried.

Senator Reeves was walking toward him, saying: "No, Dermott. Not with me in here. You've got to let me get out."

"Stay where you were," Dermott said. He meant it.

Reeves came on anyway, and Dermott whirled, catching him with a sweeping, backhand blow. It sent him reeling half the length of the room. There he stood with one hand over his jaw, looking at Dermott with stunned eyes.

"You got yourself into this, Senator. You were the smart lad with plenty of ideas, but now that the going is a little cluttered up with dead men, you'd like to rise above the whole bothersome business. Well, you're in it, and you're going to stay. You're going to stand there, and watch this traitor get shot, and you're going to keep your mouth shut."

Reeves kept wetting his lips. He was frightened. The thought of murder made him sick.

Eldad Stark kept edging inside the door. Warren started to elevate his hands, bringing them within the heat of the three-wick hanging lamp.

"Keep your hands down," Dermott said. "Well, Stark, you've been wanting this for a long time." He stopped and listened. Someone had run up the stairs. No clump of boots, but the rhythm of moving weight vibrated across the flimsy structure. Colonel Ludloe's name was spoken. An unfamiliar voice. Dermott strode to the door, jerked it open. Men were scuffling.

"Stop it!" Dermott said.

Jack Bell and another man let the fellow go. He was a half-breed, wearing a narrow-brimmed hat and fringed buckskins.

The 'breed's eyes fell on Dermott, and he started to shout: "Colonel Ludloe! He's there . . . Ludloe? I want to see. . . ."

"Sure, Steve. Of course he's here, Steve. Come in."

The half-breed stopped just inside the door. His eyes roved the room. "You fool me again! Last time you said he would soon be there, at the saloon."

"You're a Ponca scout?" Warren asked.

"Yes, Steve, the Ponca scout. I had a message for Colonel Ludloe. It was stolen from me. Yesterday. A message that the Sioux would ride this way. Today, tomorrow. Heavy Runner, Yellowtail, maybe so Sitting Bull himself, all with twelve hundred braves."

Dermott said: "Come on in, Steve. You can't go to Ludloe now. He'll shoot you when he finds out you've been drunk and lost your dispatch. I'll get you out of town."

The senator came to life and shouted to the half-breed: "You mean you're a dispatch rider for Ludloe and somebody got you drunk?"

"This man!" The breed pointed at Dermott. "And one other. They say that they would find Colonel Ludloe. But they gave me something to drink." He started to back through the door.

Dermott had drawn his gun. "No, you're not going anywhere out of here."

Senator Reeves said: "Gad, sir, you can't do this. You can't interfere with a dispatch rider."

"No? I might even end up with a dead senator. Get back!"

The Ponca whirled around and started for the stairs. Dermott's gun exploded, driving a pencil of flame across the room. The 'breed was hit but still on his feet. He got through the door, started to vault the rail of the landing.

Dermott had stepped to the hall. His gun was at arm's length. He could have shot a second before. He deliberately waited until the scout was at the crest of his leap, then he fired again. This time the bullet found its mark, and the scout crumpled, pitched head foremost to the ground.

Men had been shouting out in the hall, diving away from the line of fire, and suddenly it was quiet.

"Get him out of sight," Dermott said. He walked back inside the office, closed the door. "That's the easy way to get it," Dermott observed. "On the run. Easier than standing there, like you. Waiting. But I couldn't deny Eldad the pleasure. I've been promising it to him for too long. Oh yes, by the way, who told you there was coal underlying the Mandan area?"

"How bad do you want to know?" Warren asked.

"Not badly enough to bargain for it."

Stark showed his upper teeth in a weasel expression and said: "My arm's gettin' tired."

"All right. We've waited long enough. Ever see a man shot in the temple, Kid? One shudder, and that's the end of it. No more heat and alkali, no more forty below with the blizzard howling across these prairies. Lots of men would beat your head in for what you've done to me, but I'm not that sort. I always take the things I want the easiest way. All right, Eldad."

Warren had partly turned. His hand was against a chair. Stark was shifting his position a trifle. He wouldn't just let the hammer slip. It was too uncertain. He'd click it, and then pull the trigger. There was an outside chance.

Warren was ready to make his move. He stopped. Something whisked the air of the room. A bullet with the report rocking after it. Eldad Stark was hit. He spun, with the gun exploding in his hand. The bullet tore slivers from the floor close to the senator's feet.

Stark was still up, but his eyes were already flat, staring. Gunman's instinct made him cock and shoot again. The slug almost struck his own boots. He looked awkward and disjointed, as he took one step over buckling knees and plunged forward to the floor.

Warren had caught the flash of a rifle on the roof across the street. Perhaps Dermott had, too. Both men started at the same instant.

Dermott had spun against the wall. His hand came up with a gleam of silvered steel from the .32 Smith & Wesson. Warren dived for him. His shoulder caught Dermott waist high, and slammed him to the wall. Dermott's elbow struck, and the gun flew from his fingers, bounded to the middle of the room.

The door was open, and Jack Bell charged inside, sawed-off shotgun in his hands. He stopped. Dermott tried to rip himself away. A big man in back of Bell picked up a chair and hurled it. It struck Warren across head and shoulders, drove him down against the wall. He went down, hidden by the desk.

Warren jerked the drawer open, grabbed his gun. Bell fired the sawed-off, but the shot only ripped furrows across the desk top and slugged deep in the wall above Warren's head.

"The light!" he heard Dermott say.

Bell's second load smashed the light from its moorings and sprayed the front half of the room with kerosene. Men were plunging away.

It was dark for a moment. Dark, and the air filled with the odors of burned powder and kerosene. Then flame rose in a smoky red billow.

Warren was on his feet. "Dermott!" he shouted across the room. "Where's your fancy gun? Take your first shot, Dermott. I'll spot you this one."

A gun smashed from the midst of smoke and flame, and Warren fired back. He moved along the wall, pulling the trigger again, again. The hard buck of the gun felt good in his hand.

His voice rose in a shout: "Come and get it, lads. We're all fired up and ready for breakfast. Get your lead biscuits! One gutful guaranteed to last a lifetime!"

His eyes were blinded by flame and smoke. A shot came from somewhere amid the inferno, and his own gun answered it.

He heard Jim Swing's voice: "Kid!"

"Here, Jim."

He turned, groped, ran against another wall.

"Back this way," Jim's voice said.

He found his way inside the little sitting room. He was coughing, and Big Jim was slapping his back. No flame there, but a blind layer of smoke filled it.

"I don't need any help," Warren said. "Get your hands loaded. We've got to crowd out of here."

"I ain't got a gun."

"You're a hell of a fightin' man."

"I'm good enough to drag you out. Let's get down this hall. This whole dump will be a bonfire in two or three minutes."

Jim groped to a hall. It was dark there, but they could breathe. The blow on his head, the smoke and flame, had all combined to leave Warren unsure of himself. He kept running into the wall. They turned a corner, and suddenly there were men clustered around in front of them.

Someone realized who they were and shouted a warning. There were eight or nine men blocking the outside door. Warren sensed someone behind him and started to turn. He was slugged—down on hands and knees in the midst of charging, cursing men. He was blindly aware of the battle raging around him.

"Kid!" Big Jim bellowed hoarsely. He was in the midst of things, swinging a chair. It was knocked from his hands. Despite the wild mix-up, somebody fired. Big Jim seized a bench. It was a massive plank, a dozen feet long. He lifted it high, flung it. Its weight swept a mass of men in front of it.

Three or four were down and others charging for the stairs. Big Jim lurched after them. A man stood up in front of him, a gun in his hands. Groggily, he tried to lift it. Jim batted it away, lifted him so high his shoulder rammed the ceiling, and hurled him into the stampeding press of men in the door.

"Kid!" Big Jim bellowed again.

"What the hell do you need me for?"

Dermott's men had smashed the stair rail down, getting to the ground. Four or five were running across the freight yard. One had taken cover behind some platform steps. He rose, aimed, but a gun spoke from the warehouse roof across the way, sending him clawing for cover.

"Ha, *señores!*" Hernandez shouted. "Thees was just like running my grandfather Guzman for the post of senator from Chihuahua!"

# XV

## "HELL TOWN"

Fire raced quickly through the big, drafty warehouse, and flame lighted the town, even bringing the far bluffs of the river to ruddy relief. A mob had formed along Front Street and was moving that way. Leading it was huge, black-whiskered Buffalo Burke, a rancher from down in the Sundance country.

"Hunt your holes, you Injun-lovin' renegades!" he was bellowing. "Whar is he? Whar's the man that kilt the Ponca scout?" Someone must have told him it was Dermott, for he bellowed: "Come out here, you money-grubber, and we'll roast you in your own fire."

Warren was satisfied to lose himself in the crowd for a while. He reloaded his gun. His throat and nostrils were still raw from heat and flame.

"There's one hangin' I want to get in on," Big Jim said.

"Jim, you go over there and show them how to tie that California knot."

Dermott wouldn't be near the warehouse. He was too good at saving his own skin. Down by the river, Senator Reeves had mounted an empty hogshead and was orating. Now and then some of his words reached Warren over the hubbub of the mob. He was accusing Dermott of every perfidy known to man. The upper end of the street was deserted when he got to the Round Tent. He stepped inside. The place was empty save for one derelict asleep in a chair by the wall. He climbed stairs to the balcony, found the door to Johnny

Malette's apartment, stood outside for a while, listening. Tiny sounds came to his ears—someone moving across a padded floor.

He turned the knob, started the door swinging inward. The room was dimly illuminated by lamplight from an open door at the left. He saw Lona Pearl bent over, hurriedly stacking things in a suitcase.

She suddenly became aware of him and whirled around. "You!" she whispered. "You, boy!"

"Yes."

Her eyes darted to his holstered gun, and back to his face. He knew then that she was the one who'd squealed to Dermott, and she'd thought he'd come to kill her for it. Her dark eyes were wide.

"Why'd you do it?" he asked softly.

"You did not come to see me! You were in town, and yet you rode back to that other woman. That pale thing with. . . ."

"Never mind."

He stepped inside, closed the door. He looked at the suitcase. "Going some place?"

She didn't answer. She was standing quite stiff, her eyes looking beyond him. A scream leaped from her lips, and he wheeled, drew, fired in the same ragged instant of time.

Johnny Malette had come from a drapery-hidden door. There was a gun in his hand. Warren's bullet had a shocking power that turned him half around. The gun slid from his fingers and made scarcely a sound as it struck the padded floor. He stumbled and fell, catching himself with one hand. He lay, looking up with baffled eyes, while bloodstain sponged through his embroidered vest.

"Lona. You remember . . . that day . . . in Cape Girardeau." He was speaking without expression, lips whispering the words. "I picked you up. Washed you. Taught you all you knew. I told you then, someday I'd kill you."

His hand was in sight, dangling from the big sleeve of his coat, his long, dead-looking fingers just touching the rug. Lona must have known what was coming, but she watched with the fascination of a bird charmed by a rattlesnake. Johnny's hand had not moved, yet gun metal shone in it. He'd had a Derringer in a spring-fed sleeve holster.

Warren's Colt mixed with the Derringer, making a single crash of explosion. The bullet finished Johnny Malette, but it hadn't quite saved Lona.

Lona was hit. She was holding the left side of her breast with both hands. It was an accident that she found a chair to sit in. She was still clutching her side, with blood running through her fingers. Johnny Malette was face down, and she was staring at him.

There'd been someone in the next room. Warren sensed the movement, the slight tremble of the floor. He stepped past Lona. The door was open, light streaming in. He didn't dare show himself.

Suddenly the light blinked out, and he was in the midst of flickering blackness. He groped, touched the door casing. Gunflame tore the blackness in front of him. He fired, aiming at the flash. For three seconds the exchange was rapid, deafening. Concussion in the small room had an effect not unlike bullet shock. Warren groped forward, stumbled, fell over a padded footstool.

He rose, collided with Dermott. They clinched and reeled across the room. Instinctively they'd found each other's gun hands. Warren's gun had been forced high, while he'd thrust Dermott's toward the floor.

Warren's gun was still high. He let it drop and twisted with a sudden motion that freed his right hand. Dermott cursed. He pulled the trigger, perhaps unintentionally. The charge flew wildly across the room. For an instant Dermott was off balance, and Warren smashed a right uppercut to his jaw.

The blow snapped Dermott's head back. He pulled the trigger again, but the hammer fell with a dead snap. He swung it like a bludgeon. Warren sensed the move and caught it with an upflung arm.

Dermott's head rocked under a left and right. He reeled, his shoulders striking a wall, and he staggered forward. "No," he whispered. "No."

Warren calmly smashed him to the floor.

There were unexpected resources of energy in Dermott's body. He staggered up, reeled through the door, lurched to the stairs, tripped, fell the length of them.

He got up from the saloon floor with cigarette butts and dirt in his hair. He found the front door, flung the batwings open, and fell again from the platform sidewalk. He got up, using a hitch rack to balance himself. He kept looking over his shoulder as he reeled on into the middle of the street. He did not even realize the mob was coming back from the flaming warehouse and that he was going directly toward it.

Hoss Barbour saw him and let out a bellow. "Thar he is! Thar's the damn' Yankee that kilt my brother!"

Dermott saw them then, turned, started to run. He got fifteen or eighteen steps. Someone fired. He was hit. He got up from the dirt. Half a dozen guns exploded. He was face down in dust that looked reddish by the shifting firelight.

Warren went back inside, climbed the stairs, lighted a lamp. Lona Pearl was still sitting in the chair, holding her breast as blood thickened between her fingers.

She looked up at the Pecos Kid. "Damn you," she whispered. "Damn you . . . he was the only man alive that ever gave me anything but the dirt off his boots. And he's dead. Because I was a fool about your red hair."

"Let me see that shoulder."

Instead she reached and tangled her fingers in his hair. "You! I hate you! Kiss me on the lips before you go."

He held her against him for a long time, then he went out and spent a quarter hour finding the doctor.

He heard that Mary Coyne had ridden in with the ranchers from the Broken Arrow. Hernandez had sent her to warn them, and she'd met them only a few miles out of town.

"They're camped down by the river," Big Jim said when he found Warren in front of the Antlers Saloon.

"Who?"

"You know who. Mary Coyne, her paw, and the rest of them. I imagine she'd like to see you."

"Why would she want to see *me*?"

"You know well enough. Because she's in love with you. You ain't ridin' off and leavin' her, Kid. She's too good, and sweet, and. . . ."

"Sure, I know."

"I'm tellin' you, Kid, if you ride off and break that poor little gal's heart, there won't be enough blind cañons between here and the rimrocks of hell to hide you from Butch and me."

Warren looked up in Big Jim's eyes. It wasn't often Jim got steamed up like that. He wondered if Jim and Hernandez between them were men enough to do it, and the more he thought about it the more he decided that they were.

"Jim, if I'm fool enough to ride off and leave a girl like Mary Coyne, I hope you drag me back on the end of a lariat. And you can start looking for me up around the Musselshell."

The Yellowstone was falling with the drought of late summer, and Bill Warren had no difficulty finding a place to cross. His buckskin saddle horse, and the pack pony on its lead string, were belly-deep for a while, then they made the uncertain footing of mudbars and climbed to shelf land beyond. Warren kept on at an easy jog for half an hour, finally reining in atop the rimrocks.

He sat there with one knee hooked over the saddle horn, looking back at the lights of Miles. The prairie night had a rare purity, and he could hear little sounds, the slam of doors, an occasional shout of men, purified by distance.

He rolled a cigarette and lighted it, all without taking his eyes off the town. A campfire burned near the river. Even at that distance he imagined he could see Mary Coyne's shadow moving against it. He'd be no good for her. He'd make a hell of a husband.

He idly felt in his shirt pocket and came across the lottery ticket. It had been washed with his shirt, but the Chinese characters were still there, and the faded smears of ink covering them. He could almost hear the Chinese say: "You lucky. Red hair lucky."

For some reason, it made him laugh. Perhaps the ticket had won. He'd never inquired. He wadded it, then reconsidered, smoothed it out, folded it, stuck it beneath the band of his hat. He'd always heard that a Chinese would pay off on a winning ticket until the end of time. Perhaps, someday, he'd come back to collect.

# THE DEADWOOD DRIVE

# I

# "THE BIG TRAIL DRIVE"

There were the three of them, and they'd traveled a long way. On one side rode Big Jim Swing, on the other was Hernandez Flanagan with his guitar wrapped in a slicker behind his saddle, and in the middle was William Calhoun Warren whom few north of Texas knew by any other name than the Pecos Kid. On reaching the dusty main street of Maverly, the Kid called a halt, and sat at ease in the saddle, his hat slid back, its sweatband printed in a wet circle around his unruly, brick-red hair. The street lay quietly under the late sun of the Wyoming afternoon.

"Maverly!" breathed Hernandez Flanagan, his eyes almost closed, just the tips of his white teeth showing. "City of my dreams, weeth its gay women, its pitfalls of pleasure!"

Jim Swing, hearing him, took new interest in the town. It still wasn't much. There were thirty false-fronted buildings packed together as though, with all the Public Domain of Wyoming for the taking, these square feet were precious—and beyond just the shacks, sheds, and rubbish heaps that were common to frontier towns everywhere.

Big Jim said in a voice that was unexpectedly treble: "Gosh, Butch, it don't look big enough for many o' them pitfalls."

"So it not beeg like Dodge City and New York. So it has only seex pitfalls instead of twelve . . . we will have to visit each of them twice." He looked over at Warren. "Eh, Keed, for ninety miles with nothing but water to drink you have told

129

us of thees old friend, thees man who waited to drop in your pocket the potful of *pesos*. Where is he now with his *pesos*? He has blue eyes, thees man? He name is maybe Geneviève?"

"His name's Tom Mace, he's sixty, and he's laying low because somebody would like to shoot the top of his head off."

"A coach robber? He said where his hide-out was?"

"Yonder." With his cigarette, the Pecos Kid indicated the big, ornate, ramshackle hotel across the street. "And he's no coach robber."

"Thees place?" Hernandez drew his Colt. "A wager, *señor!* Ten dollars!"

His gun exploded atop the last word, and the bullet sped with a long lifetime of practice, smashing one of the knobs that adorned a railing on the second-story verandah.

The Pecos Kid cursed him, but there was a wild light in his blue eyes as he drew and shattered the knob next to it.

Hernandez's horse reared. He leaped from the saddle and shouting—"Twenty!"—shot out the next one.

The Kid got a second and third in rapid succession, but Hernandez's third bullet missed.

Hernandez, now miserable, sat down on a platform, drew out a black book, and, wetting a stub pencil with his tongue, painstakingly inscribed a figure.

"*Señor,* I am much in debt. To you alone, the sum of feefty thousand, four hundred thirty dollars, and seex beets."

The eruption of gunfire brought men from every doorway. One, a tall, grim-jawed man wearing a marshal's star, strode up to say: "If you Texas boys have an idea you're going to tear this town apart. . . ."

"That'd be too small a task for men o' our talents, Marshal," the Kid said with a grin that took fatigue and hardness off his face. "You're looking on three men that just took Denver apart, and they're *still* looking for the roof off Bat

McQuade's Temple Bar."

Then, telling Big Jim to keep Hernandez out of trouble, he turned his back on the marshal and walked in his saddle-sprung manner across the street.

A short, fat man with huge ears and wattles like a bull-frog's met him in the door and cried in broken German: "You know how much dot millwork cost me? Sixty cents a foot, laid down in Cheyenne, *ja,* and I had to freight it here yet. Why does everybody chop down my place mit bullets when they want target practice? What you cowboys deserve is a forkful of hay in back of the horses, not a bed in a first-class hotel."

"Sorry." The Kid looked as if he meant it. "I thought that's what you put them little knobs up there for."

"Well, ve didn't. You are perhaps looking for a room?"

The lobby was dim, filled with the musty smell of floor oil. The Pecos Kid stood in the door for a while, letting the sun-brightness get out of his eyes. Then he followed the German across to a desk flanked on both sides by dusty, potted palms.

"Tom Mace staying here?"

The man had his back turned. He flinched as though the words had force when they hit him. "Tom Mace!" He turned and let both his beefy fists strike the desk in unison. "You ask me about *Tom Mace*. I ask you who is going to pay the two days' room rent he left owing?"

Mace had never run out on a chippy debt like that in his life. Pecos was about to say so, but he sensed something was wrong. With his eyes, and with his expression, the German was trying to tell him something. A man was seated by the front window, listening.

Pecos didn't turn immediately to look. He examined the burned-out end of his cigarette, snapped a match to light on his thumbnail, and turned quite casually while applying it to the cigarette. The man was spare and rocky-faced, with high

131

cheeks and small eyes. His holster was tied down gunfighter-style on his right thigh.

The Kid turned back again. Placing himself so the gunman couldn't see what he was about, he drew from his shirt pocket a letter from Mace that the stage driver had delivered to him at Point of Rocks. He unfolded it one-handed, placed it for the Dutchman to read. Then he drawled to fill up time.

"Tom's sure enough a crook. Owes me eighty in trail-drivin' money since last August, and any man that'll beat you out of trail-drive money is next thing to a carpetbagger. I was hoping to catch him here and collect."

Pecos returned the pencil-scrawled note to his pocket, and the German, without changing position, lifted from under the counter a key wired to a big wooden tag. Holding it carefully, so the key wouldn't jingle, he slipped it inside the Kid's shirt. His face had been florid, then pale, and now florid again. Sweat glistened on his broad cheeks. He took a very deep breath, and blew it out.

The Pecos Kid drawled: "What was Tom doing here, anyhow? Last I heard, he was running a little haywire spread down by Bear Creek, buying fallen stock off the trail herds."

"He vas . . . mit trail-herd outfit." The German was having a hard time getting words through his lips. He was afraid of the gunman. So afraid he was sick. The Pecos Kid knew how it was. He'd seen times like that himself. "He . . . haff some trouble. *Ja.* Got shot . . . through hips. Mine bed he slept in. Mine whiskey he drank. Then one day . . . *pfft!* . . . he is gone, and I am holding bag filled with nothings."

The Pecos Kid thanked him and walked to the bar. It was empty. He took the key from his shirt, glanced at the tag. Number 26. That would probably be on the second floor. There'd be some back stairs. He'd wait until dark.

The bartender was outside. When he came in, the Kid asked for a bottle of St. Louis beer. The bartender took a small pony glass for himself and said: "You're the Pecos Kid, aren't you? You don't remember me, but I tended bar at Corbus City all during the cattle war. I was there the day you shot it out with Nelson Spangelo in the middle of Main Street. I was there the day the militia took you, the Spaniard, and about fifteen more down to Fort Ludloe, too. What ever happened down there, anyhow?"

The Kid drank beer, looking at him and through him. "I forget. I dug a deep hole, and scraped all that ruckus inside it."

In the lobby, the gunman had shifted position and was watching him. "Who is he?" Pecos asked, indicating with a slight jerk of his head.

The bartender looked surprised that he didn't know. "That's Ed Ward."

"Live here in Maverly?"

"No, he hit town a couple days ago."

The Pecos Kid drifted down the street, ate at Hong Gim's San Francisco Beanery, watched faro at the Green Front. It was late twilight then. He stepped from the back door of a saloon, and circled sheds and rubbish heaps to the hotel.

Lamplight came from the kitchen, but the upper floors were dark. He climbed an outside stairway to the second floor, and paused inside a darkened hall to look back. A cowboy rode cut-across toward Main Street and disappeared. No one else. No one had followed him.

It was too dark to make out the room numbers. He lighted a match, found Number 26. "Tom!" he said, with lips close to the panel. "Tom, are you there? It's Pecos."

He heard movement—someone changing position in bed. Then Tom's voice. It sounded husky. "You got a key?"

"Yeah." He turned it in the lock, opened the door, stepped inside. A faint light came through the window. The air was filled with the odor of liniment. He closed the door after him. Then he saw a gleam of gun metal. Tom Mace was propped up in bed, a .45 Colt in his hand. "What the hell, Tom!"

Tom laughed with a relaxation of taut nervousness and laid the revolver on the blankets between his knees. "I thought maybe somebody'd walked you up here with a gun at your back. That damn' Kiowa would do anything."

"Who?"

"Kiowa Johnny. He was one of Mixler's handymen. I had some trouble with him. He's around, ain't he?"

"I thought Kiowa got killed at Redpath two years ago. Only gunman I saw was a fellow named Ed Ward."

"*Him!* Well, I guess he's just as bad." With a groan and a curse, Tom elbowed and squirmed to a sitting position. "Pull the shade, Kid, and light the lamp. I want to have a look at you."

The light, after long darkness, made Tom shade his eyes. He was a middle-size man. He could have been any age between fifty and eighty. His skin was cured a Spanish-leather brown, and, judging by his flecked eyeballs and scraggly whiskers, he had Indian blood.

The Kid shook his head and asked: "What the hell *is* all this?"

"It's perfectly human. I just want to live for a while, and I stand a better chance if they think I'm in Cheyenne."

"If it's just Ed Ward and Kiowa Johnny . . . ?"

"Now, Kid, don't get on the prod. I need you for bigger things than feeding lead to a couple of cheap gunmen. Open the bureau drawer. There's a couple of articles, one for you and one for me."

The bureau contained a blue-edged legal paper, and a pint of Old Haversill's bourbon.

The Kid said: "Take your choice."

"I'm no idiot. I'll take the likker."

The Pecos Kid sat down by the light and read. The paper, sealed by a notary, signified that Mr. _____, better known as the Pecos Kid, was fifty-one percent owner of nine hundred longhorn cattle bearing the Rocking A brand, then somewhere on the trail in Wyoming Territory.

"What does this mean?"

Tom Mace let the whiskey shake the chill from him and said: "It means what it says. Those cattle are half yours. Catch up with the trail herd and claim 'em. Mixler's a hungry grizzly, but he'll honor that paper. Just fill in your real name. It's Bill Warren, ain't it?"

"I'll be glad to claim your cattle for you, but half's too much."

"A half is too little. Now keep quiet, and I'll make you agree. I threw 'em in with Mixler's outfit on account of the Injuns. Now, Mix is taking his herd across the Yellerstone to Deergrass Valley, but you and *our* steers will turn off at the Belle Fourche and cross the divide to Sundance Creek. From there. . . ."

"From there, Sitting Bull's squaws will start making jerky."

"It might be, and again it might not. You make the gamble. Start out at dark and drive all night. Pocket the herd by day in one of those deep gulches, coming down from the Black Hills, and don't show till next night. You get 'em to Deadwood. Those miners have been living on beans and jack rabbit ever since Sitting Bull left the agency. A nine-dollar steer will be worth a hundred in that camp."

He rose up in bed as though he expected Pecos to contradict him. "Yes, I said a hundred! And they'll take the whole herd at that price. There's twelve thousand miners in the Black Hills, Army estimate, and nine hundred steers won't go too damned far."

The Pecos Kid grinned and said: "Why, for that kind o' scratch, they're practically in Deadwood right now."

"Good." Tom had another small snort from the bottle. "I'd give you one out of this, but the Dutchman that runs this shebang has got me rationed at a pint a day. Got an idea I'll get drunk and start whoopin' around so those gunhawks will know where to come and finish me off."

Mixler, the Kid was thinking. Mixler of the Leon, down in Texas. He could even remember the brand—Bar M, made in the manner generally referred to as an M-on-a-Rail.

He said: "You mean Mixler's out on the trail?"

"Not only Mixler. The Haltmans are drifting to new pasture, too. Carpetbaggers ruined that country, and drought finished the job. Why, that range between Red Fork and Brazos is picked clean as the floor in a Chink beanery."

"Mixler tried to kill you?"

"Oh, hell, no. I had trouble with some o' the men. Kiowa Johnny and a long-tail lobo by the name of Andy Rasmussen got the idea I intended getting Army law on 'em for a Missouri Pacific mail car robbery they pulled back in 'Seventy-Two, and so they tried to put me out of the way. I knew I wouldn't stand any more chance than likker at a Blackfeet camp meetin' if I stayed with the herd, so, when they got me through the hips in a bushwhack one night, I lit out. Sometime I'll be up and around, and I'll gun down both of them, but that can wait. I been kicking around this country for a heap of years without one gold piece to rattle against another, and, now I see the chance, I don't want to draw out of the game. You take those steers through for me, Kid. You and

Big Jim and the Mex'. You can do it if anybody can. The Mex' *is* along, isn't he?"

"Yes."

"Then put him out at the point. No Sioux will harm one hair of a crazy man."

# II

# "DEADFALL AT MAVERLY"

Warren was at Tom's room for an hour. When he came out, the last luminous light of evening had left the sky. The moon hadn't risen. He had to grope his way down the stairs and through the alley. He circled a Chinese hand laundry and came back to the street. The marshal was standing outside a saloon, waiting for him.

"Hold up a minute," he said, and walked toward him. "I've been told that you're the Pecos Kid."

"They call me that."

"Well, let me tell you something . . . we don't back up very easy at reputations in this town. We had plenty of Texas men try to take it apart, and we're still here."

"You're borrowin' trouble, Marshal." With his hat back from his unruly hair and a grin on his face, it was hard to imagine the Kid's having carved a reputation anywhere. "We shot off a few of the hotel's knobs, but, if it'd make you feel any better, you pick up the pieces, and I'll have Big Jim Swing glue 'em back on."

"I'm not talking about that target practice. I'll be so damned glad when those knobs all get shot off so they aren't a challenge to every cowboy on the wahoo. . . . What I'm talking about is that mean-ornery greaser pal of yours. You get him on his horse and get him out of town, do you hear?"

"Why?"

The *why* was accompanied by a slight narrowing of the

138

Kid's eyes, and the marshal eased the aggressiveness of his tone. "It's not for my good, or anybody's in Maverly, but for his own. He's headed for trouble, and a whole lot more'n he can handle."

"You'd be amazed, seh, how much trouble that greaser . . . as you call him . . . can handle."

"He's making love to Terry Slavin's wife. Does that mean anything to you?"

Slavin, as a gambler and dance-hall operator, was known from the Río Grande to the Yellowstone. The Kid had heard he was a gunman. He'd heard that about lots of people.

"Why, I wouldn't want anything to happen to Slavin. I sure wouldn't. Where's all this taking place?"

"At Slavin's place . . . the Dublin Bar."

They walked together toward the Dublin, a rambling, flimsy place, two years old and already warped out of shape. As Warren neared, he heard the rapid twanging of a guitar and the musical lilt of Hernandez's voice. He found himself walking in time. He wanted to close his eyes and hum the tune. That Spanish Irishman could sing. He could sing like nobody the Kid had ever heard.

*Por mi amiga señorita,*

The words came through the cool night air.

*La vida y el corazón.*

"You hear that?" the marshal cried. "Do you think Slavin's going to stand for some Mex' making love to his wife?"

There was a good crowd in the place, a combination saloon, hotel, and music hall commonly referred to as a shebang. Hernandez, near the back of the big room, was standing with one ornate boot on a chair, plucking the guitar and singing to a thin-featured, pretty woman in scanty spangles who was taking her ease, roosting on the edge of an unused card table, swinging a foot in time with the song.

"That Missus Slavin?" Warren asked the marshal. "She took off her Mother Hubbard some place along the line, didn't she?"

"What do you mean by that?"

"I mean Slavin shouldn't have his wife in this bird cage, dressed like one of the chippies, unless he expects her to be treated like one."

"This is Slavin's place. He'll do what he likes. I tell you, he'll kill a man for that. You Johnny Rebs are always complaining about us Northerners giving you a raw deal. Now here I am trying to save your hides and. . . ."

"Us Johnny Rebs can take care of ourselves." As though to prove it, the Kid let out a Rebel yell, and with Hernandez's answer ringing in his ears he walked to the bar and called for a drink. Big Jim Swing, hearing him, rushed over.

"Kid, he's headed for trouble . . . Hernandez is. That Slavin's bad medicine. He can shoot out the eye of a snake at ten paces."

"Yeah, but can he name which eye, like Hernandez?"

"It's nothing to joke about, Kid. He'll get shot dead."

Pecos had seen the big fellow in a rage tear a place like this apart practically with his bare hands, but he was sentimental, especially with Hernandez whom he liked to mother, and at this moment he was practically in tears.

"Kid, we got to get him out of here. He ain't got good sense like we have."

"Your old man owns half the cows in California . . . if *you* had good sense, you'd have stayed there with your feet under his table. Let's have a drink."

Hernandez was singing:

*¡Ay, ay, ay, ay!*
*¡Canta no llores!*

and the woman, climbing to the table, started to swing her scantily clad body in a willing but misguided imitation of a fandango.

Hernandez finished with a grand chord of all the strings and, lowering the guitar, cried: "*¡Señorita!* I have seen it in Monterey, but never like thees tonight. You are the spirit of wine. You are the gazelle of the prairie. I will kiss your slippered toe, *señorita*. I will kiss your ankle. I will kiss your knee. I will. . . ."

"Get your claws off'n her, you dirty greaser!" a man shouted.

Slavin had come inside, leaving the batwing doors flapping behind him. He was about forty, heavy and florid. A pearl-gray, hard hat rooted on the back of his head, he wore a pearl-gray vest that would cost a month of cowboy's wages, and across its front was a massive gold chain that no cowboy could have bought in a year. His coat was open, revealing the pearl butts of two long-barreled Smith & Wesson .44s.

"Eh?" cried Hernandez as the crowd scattered. "And who are *you, señor?*"

"I'm Slavin, and I don't even bother to cut notches for Mexicans."

The woman was down from the table. She screamed.

Slavin shouted: "Get away from him, Queenie. I don't want you getting blood on your new dress."

Slavin's hands dangled from long arms, the arms from sloping shoulders. He started to draw with an upward swing of his big body, straightening and taking one step back.

Hernandez, looking casual, had seen it coming. His Colt was out, aimed across his body. Crying—"A wager, *Señor* Keed."—he fired. The bullet tore along the floor, leaving Slavin's boot sole in shreds, and sent him reeling. From the bar, the Pecos Kid drew and blasted the heel of Slavin's other boot.

The twin bullet shocks, coming from crossed directions, knocked the saloonkeeper's feet from under him and left him momentarily baffled. One of his guns had fallen; the other was pinned under him.

Jim Swing said: "Let's get the hell out of here."

The place, after a few seconds of shock, was in turmoil. A bartender came up with a double-barreled shotgun, but men blocked him at the end of the bar. Others, employees of Slavin's, were among the card tables. Big Jim charged, hurling lesser men from his way, seized Hernandez by the arm, and started dragging him to the rear door.

"My guitar!" cried Hernandez.

"I got it."

The Pecos Kid followed with his gun still drawn, on the look-out for someone who might have found a vantage point on a table or along the stairs.

Hernandez, still trying to get free, was saying: "Your solicitude ees very touching, *amigo*, but you are pulling my arm out by the roots."

"I ain't going to let you get killed. Not with all that money owing me."

Darkness stopped them for a few seconds. A cellar had once been dug back of the Dublin, and now it was half filled with ashes and empty bottles. A catwalk had been built on prop poles between the cellar and the rear of the building. They hurried along it and cut back toward the street.

People ran past them toward the Dublin Bar. "Where are

you taking me?" Hernandez kept asking.

The Kid said: "We're getting out of town."

"Do you theenk I will let that Irishman chase me from town? I am an Irishman too, *señor,* the half part of me, though whether the best or worst part I do not know."

"You've inherited the worst traits of both races. Anyhow, I don't give a damn for Terry Slavin. Something else has come up. Do you want to stay a no-good saddle bum all your life?"

"I don't know about Butch," Big Jim said in his treble, "but I want to get rich."

"What fool talk is thees? Are you not both put down in my little book for perhaps feefty thousand dollars? And is it not true that I, Hernandez Pedro Gonzales y Fuente Jesús María Flanagan, always pays his debt?"

Jim said: "Oh hell, Butch, I know you mean well, but where'll you ever get that much money?"

"One day in the faro game, it will be like thees. . . ."

The Kid said: "I'll tell you how you'll get the money. We have a half interest in nine hundred longhorns trailing east of here, and, if we can put 'em in Deadwood without leaving our hair on Sitting Bull's medicine stick, even Hernandez can pay off his debts."

"Ha, now *you* are fooling, *Señor* Keed. There is not in all Wyoming Territory enough *pesos* to pay up the debts of Hernandez. For my debts have both my father's and my mother's people keek me out. For my debts have I fled Coahuila and Chihuahua both. Has ever been a man burdened down with debt as your poor Hernandez?"

The Kid asked Jim where he'd left the horses. Jim guided them across the W-M Wagon Freight yards toward a feed stable.

The Kid looked careless as usual, but he'd been on the look-out for trouble since leaving Tom Mace's room. When

143

neither Kiowa Johnny nor that hard-eyed gunman, Ed Ward, was around, he'd felt a strong premonition of danger. A quarter way across the yard, his eyes caught the moon glimmer of blued steel, and he reacted instantly, ramming Jim one way and Hernandez the other, himself diving forward to the hard-baked earth.

Gunfire from two points tore the night with flame and concussion. He felt the wind-roar of lead as it passed closely over him. His gun was out, but he checked the impulse to fire back. His own movement, the divergent points of flame in the dark, for a moment baffled him. He was on one knee, when the guns blasted a second time.

This time he pinned them down. He fired as fast as his thumb could hook the hammer, fired on the move, from one knee, from a standing position, from one knee again.

The Kid ended in the partial protection of timbers supporting the W-M water tank. No shooting now. A wooden-bladed windmill was turning with a dismal creak. Night or day, the wind always blew in Wyoming. Water dripped on him. On one knee, he punched empty cases from the magazine and reloaded.

He'd left his own gunsmoke behind, and now it blew past him with a sulphury odor. His eyes, searching the shadows, could see nothing of the ambushers. Big Jim and Hernandez, he knew, were in shadow behind some shattered barrels and packing cases.

They'd picked a suicide spot. A bullet could cut through the whole flimsy mass.

He was ready with his gun loaded. He circled the tank, the long watering trough. The freight shed with its high loading platform was about forty steps away. With his gun poised he sprang into the open, covered the distance with long, running strides.

He was met by a volley from beneath the platform. Darkness and his own movement saved him. He dropped to one knee by one of the piles that supported the warehouse and fired back at their powder flashes.

"Jim!" he shouted while his body rocked with the gun. "Get the hell out of that rat's nest!"

He was fired empty. He moved back, again punching out the empties. Powder fouling made the ejection mechanism hard to operate. He glimpsed Jim as he circled the rear fence.

"Where's Hernandez?"

"That damned greaser! You know what he did? Went back after his guitar! I shouldn't have let him. I should have knocked him over the head and drug him whether he liked it or not."

"Quit worrying about him. He'll live to be eighty and die in bed of rheumatism."

They waited, crouched in the shadow of the rear fence. No more sign of the ambushers. They'd probably kept retreating beneath the freight shed. Shooting had brought men from the rear doors along Main Street. Some of them shouted questions, but nobody risked his life by investigating.

"¿Señores?" It was Hernandez, coming around through the dark.

"Here."

"Ha, you see, I have rescued it." He was rubbing dirt off the guitar. He kissed it. "My sweetheart. Did you theenk your Hernandez would go away and leave you? Keed, what is happening to thees country? It is going to the dogs that they should shoot a man for playing the guitar and making love?"

Pecos said: "I don't want to hurt your pride, but *this* bushwhack wasn't Slavin's doing, and it didn't have anything to do with Slavin's wife. They weren't after you. They were after me."

"But why?"

"Nine hundred head of beef. That's just a guess. Maybe somebody else would like to try delivering it to Deadwood."

They saddled and hunted backstreets through town until the broad sweep of moonlit prairie lay ahead of them to the north.

"Just the same," said Hernandez, "those bullets came very close to my guitar."

# III

# "TWELVE THOUSAND HEAD"

They slept under the stars, and late the next day, after crossing the Chugwater, sighted a long, gently drifting haze of dust against the northeastern horizon.

The Pecos Kid regarded it with a critical eye and said: "It's the trail herd, all right, and she's a big one. Sweet name o' hell. It *is* a big one!"

"How beeg?" Hernandez asked.

"Twelve thousand, according to Mace."

"Twelve thousand head in one herd! He is a liar, I theenk."

"You picked a good distance to start calling Tom Mace a liar. If he said twelve thousand, he meant twelve thousand."

"Saints of my ancestors! Thees is then the grandfather of all trail herds. Such a herd will pick the land of Montana as bare as a new-born baby in one year."

"They'll play hell picking Montana bare in a year. You stretch all the mountains and cañons out flat and Montana'd be bigger than Texas."

At Gooding's Coulée they found water holes trampled to knee-deep ooze. Late in the evening, they crested high country overlooking the North Platte, and caught their first glimpse of the great herd. It was being bedded down, scattered for miles along the green bottoms, amid willow and cottonwood. Supply wagons had been drawn into a half circle, and the cook had a fire going. Far upstream, near a bend, were more wagons and a second fire.

Men were still riding. They could hear shouting voices. Mired cattle were still being roped and dragged from the shoal water. As they approached, they saw the carcasses of seven or eight animals drawn up on cottonwood limbs, being quartered.

"Say," breathed Big Jim. "That is an outfit!"

"It's an outfit when Mixler and the Haltmans change countries. We better get down there before dark. I'd hate to come up at night and start *that* herd to running."

"Wouldn't run from thees good, clear water," Hernandez said.

"You can't tell when a big bunch like that'll run. You can't tell when they'll stop. Remember when that Long Seven herd stampeded through Leasburg, and they had to get the railroad surveyors to find out where the townsite was?"

The river was treacherous, with a current that was broken up by mudbars. They swam and waded their horses, and got them wet and tired up the steep pitch of the far side. They'd lost sight of the camp. A man stepped from the brush with a rifle across his arm, saying: "All right, you drifters, stay where y'are. You'll get shot that way, riding in after dark."

"Why?" the Kid asked mildly.

"Injun country."

"Reckon Sitting Bull's got the paint spread pretty thin, if he's holding all the ground between here and the Little Big Horn."

"We're north of the Platte, and the boss says it's Injun country."

"Then Injun country it is, and you can use three more men."

A man somewhere beyond the brush called in a raw, suspicious voice: "Who is it, Billy?"

"Strangers. Three of 'em." Then, to the Kid: "All right, ride in and talk to him."

They threaded their way through brush, guided by the firelight. Eighteen or twenty men were sprawled in a half circle, drinking coffee. One of them, a rangy, powerful man, was walking toward them. His trousers, from long riding, stuck to the insides of his legs. He had the stiff manner of one past his middle thirties who spent most of his time on horseback. Firelight silhouetted him and struck across his face, revealing the strong lines of his jaw, his prominent nose, his high cheekbones. A gun was strapped high around his waist. Silver *conchas* decorated the gun belt and holster, making multiple shines in the fire as he moved.

"Mixler?" the Kid asked, guessing his identity. He dismounted. "I'm called Pecos. This is Jim Swing and Hernandez Flanagan."

His eyes narrowed just a little at the name Pecos, but he made no comment. "Looking for jobs? We're full up, but you're welcome to drift along for your keep."

"We got jobs." He jerked his head, indicating the herd. "Sure, right here. We're taking over the Rocking A for Tom Mace."

Mixler's face, in the long-slanting firelight, became hollow and predatory. His hands came to rest on his hips. Muscles bulged his shoulders, tightened the faded blue material of his shirt. Then his lips peeled back, and he spoke: "You're doing *what?*"

"Taking over the Rocking A. The herd half belongs to us. Here's the paper to prove it."

He drew the paper from his pants pocket and handed it across. Then, pretending not to notice the expression on Mixler's face, he ambled to the fire and said: "That coffee sure enough smells like Texas."

He'd already recognized Star Glynn, a round-faced, very blue-eyed young man who carried upwards of a dozen notches on his gun. Now he spoke, and they shook hands. "Star, I never thought I'd find you punching cows. Whatever happened to that foreman's job you held down with the Three Bar Oh?"

"You know what happened to it. You don't go on workin' for a man that's swung to a cottonwood."

Mixler, holding the paper at right angles to the fire, scanned it rapidly and folded it again. He stood set on his powerful legs for a while, thinking. Then he jerked his head in a nod. "It looks to be on the level. They're Tom's cattle. If he wants to give half of them away, that's his business. You're taking them through to the Deergrass, aren't you?"

"No, seh. I'm taking 'em to Deadwood, like Tom wanted."

Mixler said: "From here on, Sitting Bull's warriors will be following us every step to the Yellowstone. If anybody falls back from the herd, he'll be asking for a Sioux tomahawk."

"We'll take the chance, seh."

Mixler controlled himself by taking a very deep breath. Then he laughed with a hard, backward jerk of his head. "Well, I guess it's your hair, and your cows. Maybe you'll change your mind before we reach the Belle Fourche."

"I doubt it, seh."

"Let's wait and see."

They ate leavings from the stew pot, and sprawled on the ground afterward to drink cup after cup of bitter, black coffee. Besides Star Glynn, there was Rasmussen, Billy Six-Spot, and Evas Williams, all gunmen at odds with the law and heading to a new range. Others were drifters, or cowboys who'd worked for Mixler or the Haltmans down in Texas. After a while, two of the Haltman brothers came down and shook hands. From a distance, Warren glimpsed a girl on the let-down steps of Haltman's wagon and guessed that it was Lita, their quarter-breed half-sister. Farther up was another camp where the small outfits had their own supply wagons and remuda.

'Punchers kept stretching and leaving the fire to hit their bedrolls or pick up mounts from the wrangler to stand first watch. After talking about the trail, Vern Haltman, eldest of the brothers, said: "That's Tom's wagon yonder, and we sort of moved our supplies in with his. We'll get 'em out, if you want, or you can just drift like part of the camp."

"Why, that's kind of you." Warren was thinking how Vern Haltman had changed. He was no longer the arrogant son of a great land owner. He was just an emigrant, moving what he had, and dependent on Clay Mixler for most of it.

"We all take a turn at night herdin'," Vern said, "bosses and everybody. There's three of you, and thet'll break about right."

Ed Mixler had taken a horse from the remuda and came riding down with Lita Haltman. They pulled up short of the fire, and by the ruddy light the Kid had his first glimpse of the girl's face.

She was about seventeen, dark and pretty. Her tightly cinched trousers accentuated both her slimness and the breadth of her hips and shoulders. She had a certain Oriental cast of countenance. Her hair, divided in two braids that fell down each shoulder from under her flat-brimmed sombrero, made her look more like an Indian than she would have otherwise, but she was only a quarter-breed.

Hernandez, exhaling, started forward, but the Kid elbowed him back, stood, and took off his hat. By that time Mixler had brought his big roan horse between the two of them.

An idea occurred to the Kid that made him feel a little bit sick. She couldn't be interested in Mixler. He had a wife in Texas. He was old enough to be her father.

Mixler said: "From here we'll have to scout for Injuns. You boys know your way around this country better'n most, so there's your jobs cut out for you. Split up your night watch to suit yourselves. That all right?"

Pecos said in his soft drawl: "Whatever you say, seh."

When Mixler rode off with Lita, Big Jim said, half joking in his high-pitched voice: "Butch, what do you think of Pecos? I never heard him thet polite to anybody. I think that raw-boned grizzly has the fear of damnation thrown in him."

"It is the evil eye, *señor!*"

The Pecos Kid grinned as he sprawled by the fire, his hat down to keep heat from his eyes. "Facts of life, boys. I was three years in the Army. Tully's Brigade, cavalry, Army of the Mississippi. You learn things in the Army. When a man's your commander, you say . . . *yes, seh* . . . and do it. A trail herd's like that. We're going through Sioux country, and I'd rather have one poor commander, than twenty good ones. Not that I'm saying Mixler's a poor commander. In that last go-'round, a commander is good or not, depending on whether he obtains his objective."

Jim said: "According to that, Grant was a better commander than Lee."

The Pecos Kid sat up with his spine stiff as a rifle barrel. "The armies of Lee, as well as those of Beauregard and Bragg, were successful in obtaining each of their military objectives. Speaking, seh, from a purely military point of view, the Army of the Confederate States was victorious. Did you know, seh, that in the final campaign of the war, Grant lost in casualties more men than Lee had in his entire Army?"

Hernandez said: "What foolish talk is thees? In Chihuahua, each odd number year is fought the civil war. Let me tell you of my uncle, Ramón Telesforo Julio y Aldasoro de Santillo Fuente . . . we call him Ray for short . . . he is general, weeth medal from Santa Anna, saying *batallero de la libertad*. Did your Lee have such a medal . . . *no!*

"I will tell you about thees one campaign. For one hundred days, on Río Conchos, fighting every day it was not too hot, maneuvering every step like Napoléon, did my uncle lose five hundred men? Did he lose one hundred men? No! He lost *one man*. On the last week of the campaign, this one soldier, this miserable *peon*, he was bitten by the Gila monster. My uncle . . . *el general* . . . he was furious. Thees man . . . he would have been shot at sunrise, for breaking his record, but, alas, he was already dead."

"Oh, hell!" the Pecos Kid said, and got up. "I'll take the first watch."

# IV

# "WIRE FENCES"

In the remuda Pecos found some horses carrying the Tom Mace iron and, choosing a big-barreled gray, asked the wrangler to cut him out. With settlements to the north and an Army post close by, he knew there was still no Indian danger. He headed up slowly rising ground, watching for Mixler and the girl.

It was quiet, as quiet as it ever is near a great herd. Cowboys, taking it at a slow, single-footing pace, sang monotonously to the rhythm of the hoofs. Wolves howled from farther out. Fatigue made him doze in the saddle. Suddenly he came awake with the realization that someone had ridden quietly up beside him. It was the girl, and she was alone.

"Where's Mixler?" he asked, without thinking.

She sat with her head held high. Her eyes, by moonlight, looked black and angry. "I don't know. Do you want him?"

He shook his head. "You scouting for Injuns, too?"

"I was with Callie McCrae. She's been poorly for the last week."

"You mean there are women yonder at the upper camp?"

"Yes. Callie and Missus Jason."

"Kids, too?"

"The two Jason boys." Then she asked: "How's Tom Mace?" He knew that question was her real reason for hunting him out.

"He's doing well. What happened to him, anyhow?"

"The Haltmans had nothing to do with it."

"Why, I didn't guess they did."

She knew what had happened, but was unwilling to talk. He didn't question her. They rode together back to camp.

The Kid awoke at gray dawn. The vinegar-tempered cook, whom the boys nicknamed "Daddy Bearsign," was banging on a tin pan, threatening to feed it to the wolves. No one took his ease at breakfast. Coffee was drunk standing, scalding hot. There was hot bread and sowbelly. Riders kept galloping onto the camp, and Daddy Bearsign kept cursing them for kicking dirt in his cook pans.

The wagon was hitched and moving while men still ate. They washed plates and cups in the river, rode at a gallop to catch up with the careening wagon, and tossed them in the plunder box. The herd was already up, the lead steers climbing trails along the northern bluffs, and Daddy Bearsign had to get ahead of them and drive hard to make the noon campsite before the herd got there.

More and more of the herd got to moving. It climbed the bluffs in sections that joined as the morning wore on and grew hot. Dust rose and drifted in the breeze. Cattle stopped to graze, and men with goads beat them on, shouting an endless—"Hi-ha!" Faces and clothes became coated with dust. Men rode with their hats down, masked, with kerchiefs filtering air from the dust that was fine and white as unbleached flour.

Wide of the herd were the other wagons, the tandem supply wagons belonging to Mixler; Tom Mace's low-wheeler driven by young Tommy Haltman; the Haltmans' Conestoga; McCrae in another Conestoga with his sick wife in a bed on the jouncing floor; the outfits of Jason, Reavley, and Wolf Carson; wagons broken down after a thousand miles of roadless prairie, sprung-wheeled and rawhided together.

In the heat of afternoon, atop the high prairie, the herd was allowed to spread through bunch grass and sage. They made dry camp, and went on again at dawn, to some flats in a wide-bottomed coulée where bawling cattle pawed water holes to mud and drank the mud.

Big Jim said: "Trouble with a big herd. You need the whole damn' Niobrara to water 'em."

There was a meeting at the other camp, and the Pecos Kid walked there on his horse-spavined legs. When he was still fifty yards off, he could hear a man's voice raised, a querulous voice: "Then we shouldn't've come. We should have turned off atop the ridge. We'd've dry camped tonight, maybe, but next day we'd have struck the Sulphur Water."

That was Dave Jason. He was a huge fellow in his late thirties, thick-chested, with hands the size of a blacksmith's. Mixler and Vern Haltman were there, but Jason had turned away from them and was addressing his words to Reavley, McCrae, and the other small owners who were sprawled around a fire with empty coffee cups in their hands.

As Pecos approached, he could see that Mixler was furious. His face looked hollow in the underlighting of the fire. It seemed to be all nose and jawbone. He had his legs set, his hands rested against his narrow hips.

He waited until Jason had finished and said, keeping a tight hold on his fury: "Maybe you think you'd do better running this outfit, Dave."

"I didn't say that. But I got four hundred steers in the outfit, and aside from a beat-up wagon and a team o' work stock it's all I own. I ain't got any money to pay for water at Willow Crick. I ain't going to give away any of my steers to pay for it, either."

"Listen, Dave. . . ."

"No, I ain't! We should have turned northeast at the Medicine like all the other herds. I could see their trail yonder. I could see it as plain as day."

"Listen, Dave. Don't tell *me* what you're going to do. You signed up with the understanding I was captain. You signed up to do as I said. So don't tell me you'll do this or do that. Your outfit will go as I say."

Jason's fists were doubled, his shoulders sloped forward. He said hoarsely: "I'll take my stock when I please and where I please."

Mixler moved with a quickness unexpected from a man of his size. He feinted slightly with his left hand, then his right hand came up with the impact of a swinging sledge. It caught Jason flush on the jaw. He went down, crumpling on bent knees. Mixler sprang for him. He seized him by the front of the shirt, held him on limber legs, and slapped him repeatedly across the mouth. Jason's hair, long uncut, strung over his face. His mouth was open. His eyes stared off focus.

"Don't tell *me* what you'll do!" Mixler flung him away then like a discarded bundle. He hitched his pants high, revealing the power of his legs, and turned on the others. "I've seen this building up ever since we crossed the Little Beaver. I should have settled it before. But we're heading into Injun country, so I'll settle it now. I'll drive this herd over the brink of hell if I want to. If you got suggestions, you make 'em. But *I'm running the herd.*"

One of Jason's boys, an eleven-year-old called Nubbins, darted from among the wagons and got down to lift his father's head out of the dirt. Blood ran from the corner of his mouth, mixed with sweat and dirt and whiskers, and trickled onto the ground. The kid looked up at Mixler and, half crying, started to call him names.

"Ya dirty damn' killer. Ya dirty, bully-raggin' son. . . ."

Tall, red-headed Rio Reavley seized the kid by both shoulders and shook him, saying: "Nubbins, keep your mouth shut."

Jason sat up and rubbed his hands back and forth across his eyes. Mixler waited, standing over him, until he'd regained his faculties, then he went on talking, keeping a hard-jawed control on his voice. "No, I didn't turn west at the Medicine. It'd take us three days out of our way. I'm not tossing away three days and letting somebody else beat us to the Deergrass, because a bunch of lousy Kansas squatters think they can grab the only decent springs this side of the Niobrara and throw fence around it."

Rio Reavley said: "They'll make a fight of it. If they do, they'll hold us up a hell of a lot longer than three days."

"That remains to be seen." He regarded Reavley with narrow eyes. "How about it, Rio? You got any ideas about running this outfit? If you have, this is the time to say so."

"I ain't afraid of you, Clay." Reavley's eyes, traveling, rested on Star Glynn who was slouched in the shadow with one heel hooked in a wagon spoke, his thumbs in his crossed cartridge belts. "I ain't afraid of your gunmen, neither. I knew *who* you were, and *what* you were when I signed up, so I got no kick coming. I'll drift along with you. That don't mean I'll like it, but I'll drift with you."

Mixler spent a few more seconds regarding the truculent faces of the small ranchers, waiting for more voices to be raised. Then, turning, he saw the Pecos Kid. "Oh, hello, Kid. I was just going to send for you. Mind coming with Vern and me? Rio, you better come, too. We'll ride over and have a talk with those nesters. Maybe we're borrowing trouble. Maybe they'll say, come on boys, and drive your longhorns right through."

# V

# "SWEET WATER"

At an earlier day, when things were booming along the Oregon Trail, wagon trains often swung north from the Platte, and camped a few days along the springs of Willow Creek to repair wagons and fill the bellies of the stock with the rich buffalo grass that grew along the bottoms. Later the springs became a favorite camping spot for wagon trains headed up the Yellowstone Trail, and for the first herds of Texas cattle. A couple of years before, however, a group of flat-busted Kansas emigrants had settled, dammed the stream, used the precious water to irrigate spud fields and garden tracts, and erected fences of split cottonwood rails against the northward push of Texas cattle.

Topping a ridge, after an hour and a half of riding, Mixler caught sight of the place and pulled up, saying: "There it is. The sweetest water in Wyoming."

The bottoms were still about three miles away, but the moon was very bright, and a person could make out the shadow marks of fences, cutting them into irregularly shaped fields. Only one cabin was visible. The others had probably been built in the protection of the cottonwoods that stood in massive clumps.

Mixler, after some thought while he rubbed the hard bristle of whiskers on his jaw, said: "It's a sure thing they have the herd spotted. They'll be on the look-out. Might cut loose if we all rode down. I'll go yonder alone. You boys wait here."

He rode away. Big as he was, he was a graceful figure in the

159

saddle. He disappeared over a terrace of the benchland. They saw him again, much later, as he turned and followed the fence. Then he dropped from sight, and for a long time they waited, and listened.

A dog kept barking, miles away. Coyotes howled in answer. There was another long time of silence, then the barking and howling again.

Star Glynn, nudging his horse up beside the Pecos Kid, said in his smooth voice: "They'll shoot him now if they know when they're lucky."

"What's he got on his mind?"

"I don't know. I wouldn't tell if I did. Mixler don't take well to having his business spilled around."

A little later, Mixler appeared from an unexpected direction.

Reavley called to him: "No deal?"

"Sure, they'll deal. We can drive through five hundred head at a time and water at a fenced-off crossing. A small charge for the whole thing. Matter of a thousand dollars. That's damned cheap, isn't it? A thousand dollars for a bellyful of water of the Public Domain?"

Star Glynn laughed in his quiet manner and asked: "How many guns they got to back that up?"

"I only saw three men. There were ten or a dozen down in the bushes."

"What'd you tell him?" Reavley asked.

"What could I tell him? There's the guns, and there's the fence. I told him he could collect tomorrow at sundown."

Reavley cried: "If you think I got eighty, ninety dollars to pay one day's water for stock at these Wyoming water holes . . . !"

"You don't like it? Well, I don't like it, either. I don't like it a damned bit."

★ ★ ★ ★ ★

It was long past midnight, when they got back to the wagon. Mixler swung down and called: "Pecos, come here a minute."

The Pecos Kid followed him to the front of the wagon, where he reached beneath the canvas and drew out a half-full quart of whiskey. He pulled the cork and handed it over.

"How about it? You got ninety dollars to pay?"

"I haven't got *five* dollars to pay."

Mixler laughed. He waited for the bottle, had a drink. He slapped the cork tight and put it back in its old place. "They'll lower that price tomorrow."

"I doubt they will, seh. Waterin' this herd would destroy a third part of everything they got planted in them bottoms."

Mixler still smiled, but his eyes had narrowed. "What's wrong, Kid? You afraid of those sod-buster guns?"

"I ain't afraid of 'em. I just don't go out o' my way looking for a fight. Is that why you called me over here . . . to ask me that?"

"No. I wanted to know what you had against me."

"Nothing, seh."

"What'd Mace say when he signed those steers over to you? Did he say I tried to bushwhack him?"

"Why, I'll tell you what he said. He said Kiowa Johnny and Rasmussen tried to bushwhack him. He said he knew too much about some Missouri Pacific mail car robbery."

"Oh." Some of the suspicion seemed to go out of him. His manner became confidential. "You know, I been fighting to keep this outfit from splitting down the middle. There's the Haltmans and me, and there's that bunch of haywire outfits at the upper camp. You're going to have to choose between us, Kid. I think you made your choice already. Which is it going to be?"

Speaking slowly, meeting Mixler's eyes, the Kid said: "I'm like Rio Reavley. I knew you were captain of the herd, when I signed up. I knew who you were. I'd heard of you in Texas. You make the decisions. You ain't telling *me* what to do, but you can tell my cows what to do . . . from here all the way to the Belle Fourche. There . . . does that answer your question?"

There was no slight hint of a smile on Mixler's lips now. His eyes were like pieces of gray quartz above his high cheek bones. "Yes," he said. "I guess it does."

The herd was unusually quiet. It was a bad sign. Pecos lay in his blankets, staring at the stars, listening. He could hear night herders, making their rounds, singing the endless words of a trail song. He had the feeling that any unexpected sound, or less than that, even the absence of an expected sound, would start them up and running. He fell asleep, and it seemed like only an instant later when morning and the stirring camp awakened him.

The herd, through rising layers of dust, was up and moving. They rolled northward, topped the low ridge during hot afternoon, and at night, bawling for water, they were brought to a stop half a mile from the Willow Creek fence.

Cursing with each move, Daddy Bearsign emptied stale water from his barrel into the coffee pot which he suspended over a sagebrush fire. Eight or nine men had gathered for grub pile. Mixler wasn't there. None of the Haltmans was there.

"What the hell's going on here tonight?" Daddy kept saying.

Four men led by Rio Reavley rode down from the other camp. Daddy, wiping sweat from his eyebrows, looked up

162

and said: "If you're looking for water, you can go down to the crick and dip it."

Rio said: "Where's Clay?"

"He never asked me where he can go. I'm just cook here."

Vern Haltman had seen them arrive and rode up at a gallop. "You looking for Mixler? He's down in the valley making a dicker."

"Oh." Rio relaxed a little. He edged his bay broncho close enough so he could look down in the coffee pot. It had just started to boil.

Daddy said: "Well, git down and have yourself a cup. I'll have beef and doughgod maybe. And gravy thickened with trail dust. What a hell of a place to camp, right a-hind this herd. I'd like to know where everybody is. They're generally like a band of wolves this time of night."

Rio and the rest were dismounted, drinking coffee, when Mixler came. His eye dwelt for a moment on Reavley, on the purple-bruised face of Dave Jason. He said to Daddy: "Put out the fire. Get the wagon hitched." Rio started to say something, but Mixler's raw voice cut him off. "Go back and get your outfits ready to roll."

Rio said: "What the hell . . . ?"

"We've moving across . . . tonight!"

"How about those nesters?"

"They'll be paid off. They'll get every damn' thing they been looking for."

Daddy Bearsign cursed and kicked the coffee pot over on the fire. It was suddenly dark with the flame gone. Still cursing, he started to hurl things in the wagon. Grim-faced and taut-lipped, Reavley and the others rode back to their camp.

The air was lifeless and oppressive. Bullet-colored clouds had risen in the west. There was sheet lightning, distant thunder. For a while the moon shone, then it slid behind layers of clouds.

The herd was slow in bedding down. After an hour, all the wagons were hitched. At both camps, drivers waited in surly, apprehensive silence.

The Pecos Kid looked for the cook fire, found it drowned under the coffee, and Daddy Bearsign in his wagon, ready to move.

"Mixler's orders, and don't ask me why," Daddy shouted.

Pecos roped a fresh mount from the remuda. He rode along the herd until he met Jim Swing.

"What the hell's he up to, Kid? You think he'll pay any money to those nesters?"

"He wouldn't pay 'em a Jeff Davis dollar."

"He's looking for trouble. They're gunned to the teeth."

"They're looking for trouble, too. Anybody that tosses up a fence around water is looking for trouble."

"Just the same, I don't like it. There's women and kids down there."

They sat quietly for a quarter hour—for half an hour. Riders on the big circle had kept the big herd well bunched on the gently sloping hillsides. Finally they started to bed down, but thunder and the smell of water kept them nervous, impatient. One big brindle steer was up, somewhat downhill from the others, bawling in a never-ending, high-pitched trumpet.

A rider came up from the darkness, shadowy and small. It was Lita Haltman. She drew up with one of her slim movements and said: "Oh, I thought you were Vern."

Pecos could barely make out the smooth outline of her face. She had her sombrero on the back of her head, held under her throat by a tie-string, and her hair, dislodged by riding, fell in heavy masses around her shoulders. For a few seconds she sat quite straight, the buckle of her belt pressed against the saddle horn, her dark eyes on him.

Pecos asked her: "What's Mixler up to, anyhow?"

"How would I know what he's up to?" The sharp defensiveness of her voice was a surprise after the long quiet. "I haven't talked to Mixler since morning."

Pecos tilted his head at the valley, now an uncertain mass of shadow below. "Reckon he's yonder, trying to make a deal?"

"No. He's at the wagon."

She touched her spurs to the side of her horse and started away, intending to go around the herd on the downhill side, but a rider came up at a stiff jog and spoke to her.

"Stay out o' there, miss." The Kid recognized the voice. It was Billy Six-Spot, the same man who had stopped them that first night they rode into camp. "You better get back to the wagon. Vern's looking for you."

Billy rode on, his hat off, mopping sweat off his head with his kerchief. Silence settled again. It became tense; even the brindle steer had stopped trumpeting. It had the feel of a string drawn taut, of a trigger haired until the slightest breath would release it. Suddenly, from up the slope, came the sound of a galloping horse and the clanging of a tin pan being drawn on the end of a lariat rope.

Next instant, as though moved by a common mind, the great herd got to its feet and stampeded. It had been done deliberately, done at Mixler's order. The earth vibrated. It was like thunder but multiplied a thousand times. Going downhill, the dark sea of cattle split around a little knoll and rejoined, a maddened, bawling mass.

Pecos and Big Jim were caught between one end of the herd and the heavy rail fence. They spurred forward, got clear, and swung back. Dust made the air too thick to breathe. In the darkness, it was like a black fog. They sucked air through folded kerchiefs, guided themselves by sound.

A breeze sprang up, carrying the dense layer of dust away from them. Lightning kept flashing closer, and there were big droplets of rain. The lead steers, outdistancing the others by a hundred yards, had been turned by the heavy rail fence. Men were below, in the bottoms, shooting. Through dust, the powder flames were ruddy, out of focus. Then the main herd bore down, swept the fence before it, washed in a dark wave across the valley.

Sounds of the herd were suddenly far away. They could hear the shouts of teamsters, getting the wagons rolling.

Hernandez found them. They fell in with other riders. Ahead of them was the cook wagon, bounding wildly across the rough prairie as Daddy Bearsign stood and whipped the team. The Haltman wagon was at his left, and farther away, approaching at a ten or twelve degree angle, were the wagons from the other camp.

A group of Mixler's men, half a mile to the west, had reached the fence and were met by a scattering of gunfire from the bottoms. They rode on, whooping and shooting, but real opposition failed to present itself. What defense the sod busters had was trampled or put to flight by the herd.

A cabin, abandoned with a kettle still boiling on the stove, had stood in the midst of the stampede, but sheds and clotheslines and a neatly fenced garden plot had all been pulverized beneath a thousand hoofs. Hungry, thirsty cowboys went inside, drank the hot water from tin cups, and started going through the cupboards, but Mixler rode up, leaned to look through the door, and said: "Put that stuff back. We're not robbing 'em. We're just watering the herd."

By dawn, the wagons, with barrels filled, had scaled the northern slopes. For hours there'd been intermittent gunfire. It increased as daylight came. A group under Star Glynn fought a rear-guard action as the herd moved, unwillingly at first, then in long, snake-like columns up the draws to benches, and to the high prairie beyond.

# VI

## "WHIPSAW TRAP"

By noon Willow Creek, with a third of its houses and half of its irrigated fields in ruin, lay over a ridge, out of view. Here the grass, untouched by trail herds, grew deep, so wind currents made wave-like shadows in flowing across it. The herd slowed and spread out, grazing its way, and Mixler brought the wagons to a stop. It was grub pile, after almost twenty-four hours of hunger.

"Thees was pretty rough trick, no?" Hernandez asked, coming to squat behind the Pecos Kid with a plate of beef and dumplings in one hand and coffee in the other. "Some of these people lose everytheeng, just for to save two, three days on the way to Montana. Perhaps not even thees, for now we have rough country ahead, and will have to turn west anyway. I theenk perhaps one day I will shoot thees Mixler through the heart."

The Kid spoke without turning his head. "It was pretty rough. But this is a pretty rough country."

"You theenk he did right?"

"I didn't say that. But he's boss. On the trail you have *one* boss. You do what he says, whether you like it or not."

"But all the same, there had better be no more Willow Creeks."

"There won't be. From here on the country belongs to Sitting Bull or anybody who has enough guns to claim it."

There was no trouble during the night. The herd went on,

through days of heat. A "dry rain" rose in the west almost every afternoon with black clouds, thunder, and once or twice a cooling draught of moisture. There was water at Claus Coulée, at Henderson Creek, at the Niobrara. The country became rough, gashed by steep-sided coulées running northeastward toward the Black Hills.

Night and day, Pecos, Jim, and Hernandez scouted for Indians. There were signal smokes and some cold sign, but nothing to give much alarm. Sitting Bull was said to have most of his forces to the north and east of the Black Hills, trying to cut off supplies from the gold miners.

At night, when they rode in, they could sense discontent rising among the small outfits. Mrs. McCrae was sick and getting worse. The wagon under her was beaten to pieces by the rocks and gully crossings of the route Mixler had chosen. Below, to the west, one's eyes could rove the flat prairie generally chosen by trail herds, where a wagon could roll easily, mile after mile, without a pitch or a draw, but Mixler kept swinging away from it.

On the third night from Niobrara, with men sprawled in the heat of Daddy Bearsign's fire, there was a jingle of bridle links, and six men from the other camp rode up. Reavley was scared of Mixler, like almost everybody else, and to keep from showing it, he made his voice aggressive and brassy. "What the hell you trying to do, Mixler, put us all afoot?"

Mixler took time to finish picking his teeth. He snapped his clasp knife shut and turned. He looked at Reavley, and beyond at Jason and McCrae, and gray-whiskered Wolf Carson. "No, I'm not trying to put you afoot. And I'm not worrying about it, either. These cattle are what I'm worried about. I'm taking 'em by the shortest route, and I'm taking 'em through the best grass. The best water. You follow any way you can. If your wagons give out, try riding on horseback.

Maybe you'll end by crawling on your bellies. That's your look-out."

"We got kids along. McCrae's wife's sick."

"Nobody asked Jason to bring his whelps, nor McCrae his wife."

"Damn it, though, when there's an easier way to the west. . . ."

"If you knew an easier way, you should have taken it and not joined up with me."

Reavley started to shout back in anger, but Gayle McCrae, a beat-out little man, was in ahead of him. "Is it too much if a man asks where you're headed?"

"No. I'll tell you where we're going. Right now we're headed for the upper Warbonnet. We'll cross it by the old Fur Company Trail."

"How about Windham Coulée?"

"We're crossing that by the Fur Company Trail, too."

"There ain't crossing *there* for a wagon."

Mixler's voice had become deadly. "Who told you that?"

McCrae hesitated, but Wolf Carson said: "I did."

"You the one that's behind all this dissension, Wolf?"

Reavley shouted: "No, he's not. I'm the one behind it, if you want to know. You've taken the tough road instead of the easy one ever since we left the Little Beaver. When Tom Mace objected, you tried to kill him. When Jason said something, you beat him half to death with your fists. Well, by the gawds you ain't scared *me* out. I'll say what I think. It's this . . . you're trying to make it so almighty tough no wagon can follow you. You think because there's women and kids along, we'll have to shuck out. You think you can make us do it one after another and drive the whole shebang through to the Deergrass all by yourself."

He was backing away as he talked. Mixler, rangy, with his

bull neck and powerful shoulders sloped forward, followed him. Rage had turned Mixler's face an ashen color under his tan. His arms had thickened, tightening the denim material of his shirt. His hands at the ends of long arms were stretched down.

Looking casual, the Pecos Kid stood up. He backed away from the fire a trifle. His eyes swung to the shadows. He saw Andy Rasmussen, gangling, stooped, his hand half lifting his Colt from its holster. There were others, a man on each side—Star Glynn and Evas Williams.

"Man behind you, Reavley," he said softly.

His voice jarred the long, taut seconds of silence. Reavley had been ready to draw. He checked himself, spun, and saw Rasmussen. He saw the others. He got his hands high.

"I should have known you'd be set up to kill me when I rode over here, Mixler."

Mixler, gaunt from fury, had turned on Pecos. Vern Haltman got hold of his arm.

"Clay! Use your head."

He shook himself free. Instead of saying anything to Pecos, he turned back on Reavley. "All right, Rio. If you and your friends don't like the way things are going, you can get out."

"That suits us. We'll start cutting our stock in the morning."

"You'll not cut out a steer. If you go, you'll go and leave your cattle behind. I'm not holding this herd up a day or an hour."

When they were gone, the Pecos Kid went back and picked up his coffee. It was half cold. He drained it, tossed away the grounds. He knew everyone was looking at him. Big Jim had moved over and was standing slightly at his left. Hernandez was somewhere in the shadow of the wagon.

Mixler hitched his pants up, a characteristic movement that showed the stud-horse power of his legs, and was about to speak, but there was a quiet movement at one side of the wagon, and he saw that Lita Haltman was standing there, listening.

"You got something to say, Mixler?" the Kid asked in his quiet drawl. "If you have, let's get it settled now."

"I was thinking maybe you liked those quitters up there." He jerked his head, indicating the other camp. "If you do, maybe that's where you should be camping."

"Maybe it is. We'll be needing our wagon. You're hauling supplies in it, you know."

Andy Rasmussen, slouching over to the fire, swished the coffee back and forth to see if a cupful was left among the grounds. There was a smile on his long, loose face. He put the pot back and looked over at the Kid.

"I heard what you said to Reavley. What'd you mean . . . that I intended to shoot him in the back?"

"I heard some place," the Kid said softly, "that you'd picked up a notch or two that way. They told me that . . . down in Fort Addison."

Rasmussen was still leaning over. The cup was in his left hand. In straightening, his right hand suddenly swung up for the six-shooter that rode low in a holster on his thigh. He'd telegraphed it with his eyes, and Pecos, faster by a fifth of a second anyway, had him hopelessly beaten.

Pecos drew with a backward, dragging slap of his hand. He hesitated a fragment of time. Then the gun came to life lashing flame and lead across the fire. He'd resisted the temptation to kill Rasmussen. Instead, he aimed at his wrist. With ten steps separating them, with Rasmussen strongly revealed by the fire, it was an easy shot.

The slug struck his forearm. Force of it turned him

halfway around. He was still up, reeling and glassy-eyed. He fell to his knees, grabbed his bullet-ripped arm, and stared at it as blood ran in swift streams from the tips of his fingers.

For a shocked second, nobody moved. Pecos stood straight, his gun drawn, the barrel elevated a trifle, a wisp of powder smoke trailing from it.

"I'm not looking for trouble," he said in a clear voice. "All I want is to get to Deadwood with nine hundred steers. Maybe I'll do it, too. Me and my friends. If you had any idea of getting rid of me the way you got rid of Tom Mace, you better send somebody better'n Andy around to do it. And I'll give you warning right now. Next one, if I'm lucky enough to outdraw him, is going to need more'n a bonesetter. He's going to need a man with a shovel."

He laughed, when he finished. He didn't seem to be particularly wary of anyone, but he didn't lose track of Mixler and Star Glynn. Those, he knew, were the dangerous ones, and for the moment that danger had passed. They wouldn't try anything—not tonight, anyway.

# VII

## "THREE DEAD MEN"

The following evening, Ed Ward and Kiowa Johnny rode in from the direction of Maverly and immediately had a private talk with Mixler.

Hernandez said: "Keed, those were the gunmen that followed Tom Mace?"

"Yeah. They were in Maverly. Wonder if they ever got a bullet in him. I'll lay gold against Jeff Davis paper that they didn't."

"Perhaps, but one thing is for certain, they will try to put bullets in *us*. One at a time, they weel try to keel us. In the dark, in the back. They are afraid of you, now that you outdrew Rasmussen. We had better stay together, or we will not be three happy men riding to Deadwood. We will be three dead men riding nowhere."

There had been Indian smokes to the east and the northwest, so most of the next days were spent scouting for Sioux. They returned early one afternoon as the herd approached Windham Coulée.

Windham Coulée was a mighty gash, from one to four miles in width, sundering the country that sloped down from the Black Hills. Actually, it was not a single watercourse, but a network of them, diverging and joining, leaving hills with cutbank sides that rose flat-topped to the level of the high prairie. Many years before, the fur traders had scratched out a cart trail to the bottom, but it had eroded, and streams, following its ruts, had cut new gullies, many to a depth of six feet.

Daddy Bearsign, getting there hours ahead of the herd, had drawn up and was spitting tobacco juice over the first cutbank pitch when Pecos and his companions rode up. In a minute Fred Jardine drove up in Reavley's wagon.

Jardine said: "McCrae'll never make it to the bottom. That wagon he's driving is just loose boards tied together with rawhide. And that Pittsburgh of Jason's ain't much better. Why, that old Pittsburgh came to the country durin' the Mexican War."

Ellis Haltman drove up in the supply wagon and, without stopping, started along the rims looking for a new course to the bottom. McCrae and Jason straggled along in their beat-up wagons half an hour later.

McCrae, without saying anything, sat hunched and dejected in the seat, looking into the coulée depths.

Pecos rode up beside him and said: "Hello, Mack. How's your missus?"

He shook his head, saying—"Oh, tol'able."—in a manner that showed she wasn't tolerable at all. "She's sick with what her sister had. The gallstones. Sometimes, along the gumbo patches, it's smooth enough to sleep, but it pains her to get jounced around." He motioned into the wild depths of the Windham. "She'll sure as hell get jounced down there."

"If I was you, I'd drive that woman back to Cheyenne," Daddy said. "They got a doc there, a Chinaman, and he treats them bowel stones with some sort of dried leaf he gets all the way from Frisco. I had a pal one time . . . he was camp cook when the U.P. was building . . . and he had bowel stones so bad he was doubled with his knees higher than his ears and even whiskey wouldn't help him. Well, that Chink stewed up some of that green stuff that got him limbered and sound asleep, and two days later he shucked them stones, a handful of 'em like the marbles you use playin' kelly pool, and he ain't had an attack since."

The thin face of Callie McCrae appeared in the opening of the Conestoga. She was probably no more than thirty-five, but she looked fifty. Seeing her, Daddy Bearsign took off his filthy, dusty hat.

She asked: "Who was this doctor?"

"Called himself Hung Gow, or something like that."

McCrae said with an angry defensiveness: "We can't go back there."

She was ready to cry. "Why can't we, Gayle? Why can't we turn around and go back to Cheyenne?"

"Because the wagon would never hold up. The wagon wouldn't get us back to the Platte."

She pointed at the coulée. "How long'll it last down there?"

He said doggedly: "We'll get through somehow, if we stay with the herd. If our wagon gives out, we'll travel with Reavley. I'll get you to Miles. There'll be a doctor in Miles. Maybe a Chiny doctor, if that's what you need."

The Kid wondered if she'd live that long through the abuse of this foothills trail. It would be hell from here on, following this rough country. It still wasn't too late to turn west, reach the flat going past the headwaters of the Powder.

The herd, not on the graze, had topped a hump of the prairie a couple of miles away. Soon some riders came in sight and cut across toward the supply wagon. From half a mile distance, Pecos knew that one was Mixler, another Lita Haltman.

Mixler and one of the men dismounted and descended into the coulée. In a few minutes, Ellis Haltman rode part way to the main group of wagons and signaled them with his hat. When they arrived, they saw Mixler and Vern Haltman, following a narrow bench along the steep coulée side about three hundred feet below.

Fred Jardine said: "They expect us to go down *there?* Holy hell, that's not track enough for a bighorn sheep."

From inside the sheets of McCrae's battered Conestoga came the sobbing voice of his wife. "Gayle, you know what he's trying to do. He's trying to wreck our wagons and kill us all. I told you at Brazos how it'd be. Them big outfits like Mixler and the Haltmans never had any interest in poor folk except to kill 'em off for their own profit."

Lita Haltman heard her and stood up in the stirrups to cry: "That's not true!"

"It's true, and you know it's true!"

"Callie!" McCrae said. "Let's not have any more of that. Lita's always been nice to you."

Mrs. McCrae started to cry. The Pecos Kid tried not to hear her. It made him feel sick and sweaty. He wanted to help her, but there was nothing he could do. Just *nothing*. This was Indian country. They couldn't turn back. They had to go on, across Windham, across other coulées as bad. If the wagon fell apart, they'd have to double up. If all the wagons fell apart, they'd have to ride, or walk, or crawl, or die.

Lita rode over and said: "Pecos, you're going to Deadwood?"

"That's my idea."

"Couldn't you take her along?"

"I don't know." Through Indian country, without roads, it would be impossible, but he couldn't bring himself to tell her it was impossible. "We'll have a look and see."

Mixler, climbing the steep coulée, was watching them. Lita saw him, and her hands froze on the reins. Color had risen in her cheeks, beneath her natural pigment, beneath her tan. They were often together, she and Mixler, but up till then Pecos had thought it was Mixler's doing. Now he wasn't so sure. Lita was just a kid. Mixler was old enough to be her father. He had a wife in Texas, and a boy almost as old as Lita.

Hernandez jogged up and sat slouched forward, a thoughtful smile on his lips. "You theenk perhaps?" He jerked his head down the steep slope at Mixler. "You theenk she could care for heem . . . that man?"

"I'll kill him first!"

"Now, *señor,* you speak like the Spaniard, like the son of a don. I have sat watching you these many days. Each day eet come a little closer. Each day more plain that *one* day you will kill that man, or he will kill you."

The Kid knew it was true. He'd sensed it from the first hour. He'd been sure of it since the night he outdrew Rasmussen.

He heard Hernandez shout, "A snake! Is it a wager, *señor?*"

He turned in time to see Hernandez lean back and to one side unholstering his Colt. He fired, and a rattlesnake came twisting from a sage clump, throwing loops in his thick, scaly body.

The Kid drew a second later and tried to cut the rattles, but the tail was in lashing movement, and his bullet pounded a geyser of dirt, missing by an inch. He fired again, but the rattles hung by a shred of skin, and it took a third shot to free them.

Hernandez was jubilant. "Slowly do I free myself of debt!" He had out his stub pencil and little black book. "Behold, now do I owe only the feefty thousand, four hundred dollars, and seex beets!"

Mixler wheeled his horse at the sounds of the shooting and rode toward them. He was stiff-spined, with his powerful legs rammed hard in the stirrups. His eyes traveled to the snake that still had a twist of life in him. He grabbed his gun, rammed it forward as though to add his own strength to the force of the bullet, and fired, blasting the snake in half. Ponderous as he seemed, the man was swift with a gun.

"What does that do for me?" he asked with a downward twist of his lips.

"No-theeng, for you did not wager."

Mixler rode back, poking the empty cartridge case from his gun. With it still in his hand he waved toward the coulée and shouted: "All right, get a move." He called to Tommy Haltman with the supply wagon. "You go first. Lock the hind wheels. Skid to the first reef. We'll be down there to help you along."

The wagon was built low to the ground, with wide, solid wheels that made it a rough rider across the bunch grass of the prairie but added to its durability, giving it a low-slung center of gravity. It took the first steep pitch, its hind wheels snubbed with a hickory pole, then the pole was removed, and it found a twisting, turning switchback from one rock reef level to the next to the final cutbank descent.

There, after some wrangling between Tommy and his elder brother, the team was unhitched, a post was set in a rock crevice, and the wagon was lowered, tailgate first, by means of doubled lariat ropes. The descent had taken half an hour, and the first steers were along the crests, bawling, sniffing the air for the smell of water.

"Get them wagons started down!" Mixler bellowed. "Get 'em started before that herd tramps out what road we got."

The cook wagon was next. More ungainly and top-heavy, it clung precariously to the switchback. Then came the Haltmans' wagon, and Reavley's, and Jason's.

Jason's wagon took the first descent in a cloud of dust and

came to a stop with one of its front wheels sprung. Jason got his team turned. Someone had removed the snubbing pole. He kept going along one of the switchback turns. His hand brake was useless. The pitch became steep, letting the wagon overrun his team. They lunged and ran with the wagon careening on its wobbly wheel, hanging to the edge of the reef. Still, it might have escaped disaster, but for the crippled wheel. The wheel crumpled inward, and the wagon overturned. It struck on its side.

A rock projection stopped its descent momentarily. Jason had fallen free. He scrambled to his feet with the reins still in his hand. Supplies rolled from the rear of the wagon. A barrel of flour broke.

The horses were tangled and lunging to their feet. They'd have killed each other, but Gonzales, a little, dehydrated Haltman 'puncher, risked his life by cutting the tugs. The wagon commenced sliding now that the tugs were gone. It turned over and over, smashing itself, and ended a demolished mass of rawhide and warped boards in the bottom.

McCrae had been following the Jason wagon. His face looked haggard, grayish under its tan. His wife was in the back, calling to him.

Pecos, riding along the steep side, came up at the rear of the wagon and saw her lying on her back with both arms across her face.

From below, he could hear Mixler shouting: "Well, get her out o' there and get that wagon moving. We don't want to be trapped in this coulée, eating the drag of the herd for two days. Damn you, McCrae, get that wagon to rolling, or we'll go and the hell with you."

Pecos tried to talk to her, but she stopped up her ears and kept wailing: "Leave me alone! Go and leave me alone! I don't care if I die. I'm not leaving this wagon."

Pecos called to Jim Swing, who dismounted, lowered the end gate, and, leaning inside, lifted her out. He kept talking to her like he'd talk to a child as he carried her, half sliding, half walking, all the way to the bottom.

The Pecos Kid, preceding him, caught up with Tommy Haltman. "Get those supplies unloaded. We'll have to make a bed for her."

"Hold on! We can't unload this. . . ."

"That's my wagon, and we're going to unload it. Some of this stuff can go in the cook wagon, and some in your own."

Mixler rode up as he was speaking. He stopped his horse, spat balled-up saliva and dirt, and said hoarsely: "I'm giving the orders here, Pecos, or have you forgotten?"

"If you're giving orders, tell young Haltman to unload the wagon or I'll kick that stuff out on the ground."

Mixler looked at him, and at Big Jim, who still held the woman. Lita, riding a wiry little gunpowder roan, was approaching at a gallop, and perhaps it was she who made him change his mind. "All right, Tommy. Swap some of that cargo. Make room for her."

Men were carrying supplies downhill to lighten McCrae's wagon. Besides food, there were odds and ends of furniture, an old trunk filled with linens and fancywork. Lightened, and with men helping, it made the descent on its creaky wheels.

Steers were coming now, forty or fifty already at the bottom. Riders fought to turn the main body of the herd back so wagons could get going and not be trapped in the drag.

The bottom broadened. There were groves of cottonwood. A spring-fed stream flowed from one of the feeder gullies, but already it had been turned to mud by the herd. The lead steers had stopped, and others were piling in on them, and the wagons went on alone to another spring, flowing clear and cold from an undercut strata of sandrock. There, by working through the night, they got McCrae's wagon repaired. His wife returned to her flat pallet on the bottom. The wagon set out with the others at dawn, but the coulée bottom became a hell of rock and gullies, and in the afternoon one of the wheels buckled. It was repaired somehow, rawhided, pegged. It gave out again on a steep pitch, and the sagging shock took the opposite wheel with it. The wagon was hopeless. Some of the belongings were saved, loaded in with Jason's.

They kept going, hard pressed by the herd.

Returning at night with Jim Swing and Hernandez after a day of scouting for Indian sign, Pecos called McCrae to one side and said: "Your wife can't take it any more, Mack. I think you'd better head for Fort Lodgepole. Take our wagon and that big team of grays. You can make it in forty-eight hours."

"How about my cows? There's only four hundred of 'em, but they're all I got in the world."

"We'll cut 'em out with ours and drive to Deadwood. If you're lucky, it'll make you a fortune."

"Mixler'll never let you do it. *You* ain't driving to Deadwood. Nobody is. That Rocking A stock will go all the way to Montana whether you like it or not. Mixler won't let anybody split the herd now it's this far."

"Let us worry about that. You better head for Lodgepole."

"I want to think it over. I don't know what to do."

It was half a day's work finding a road over the side of the coulée. Beyond lay more rough country, well watered, deep in grass, but a teamster's nightmare. McCrae took one look at it and made up his mind.

"All right," he said to Pecos. "I'm ready to go."

Mixler shrugged, when told of their decision. He gave the appearance of not caring one way or the other, but as he turned away, Pecos could see satisfaction in his manner. He'd driven off one of the small owners. Jason would be next. And then Reavley, or Carson, or even themselves.

# VIII

# "SIOUX COUNTRY"

Jason's wife prepared them an early supper, and they set out, McCrae driving with an extra team tied to the end gate, and Pecos, Hernandez, and Big Jim ranging the country on the lookout for Sioux. They traveled all night, following the old travois trail to Big Muddy Springs. There, swapping horses, they headed across vast flats to the southwest.

In the afternoon they sighted a freight outfit, a string of twenty wagons creeping northward along the Army road. The boss, a rough, red-headed man, offered McCrae the protection of his outfit as far as Tongue River Post. Fort Lodgepole, he said, had been abandoned in the face of Indian pressure.

Returning the next day, Pecos and his partners found the herd deep in the bottoms of Eaglerock Creek where Jason's wagon was in ruins and Reavley's a three-wheeled cripple. After a night of work, hacking spokes from green cottonwood, Reavley hitched up and started out with the rest, but one of the wheels went out of line and collapsed inside half a mile. Jason, who had moved his outfit in with Reavley, sent his son Nubbins ahead to ask for help from the Haltmans.

Vern was driving the big wagon. He stopped and gave thought to the boy's request. "We have an extra wheel forward in the cook wagon," he said, and was on the point of saying yes, but he saw Mixler coming on the gallop.

Mixler pulled his big gray horse to a stop amid a shower of dirt and addressed the boy roughly. "You looking for help on

184

that broken-down wagon? Well, go back and tell your dad and Reavley that they won't find it here." When the boy, scared and almost ready to cry, had turned and ridden off, Mixler said: "I don't know how many times I got to tell 'em these things."

Vern, fighting down an angry tremble, said: "It's either lend them a wheel or let them drop out."

"Then they drop out, and to hell with them. They been a stone around our necks ever since we crossed the Nations."

He'd have ridden away with that, but Vern stopped him. "Clay!"

"Yeah?"

"You know what they'll say about us if we show up with cattle and no owners. It looks like a poor way to start in business in a new territory."

"You're a tender-hearted fellow, Vern. You always had plenty of mercy for everybody. That's why you ended over your tail bone in debt and needed me to bail you out. Now, this herd's being run my way. I'll dump those Block H cattle of yours on the Deergrass. When I do that, I'm through, and you'll be free to go broke the same way you did in Texas. *When we get to Deergrass,* that is. You're a good boy, Vern, so let's talk no more about it."

The herd left Reavley, the Jasons, and Wolf Carson far behind. When Pecos and his companions came in at dark, they found them at work, cutting the broken wagon down to a cart. Two-thirds of the cargo was thrown away. Clouds had been slowly gathering all day, and it rained. The rain was fine and cold, slowly soaking all of them.

At noon they'd stopped to eat cold beef and dummy, when Mixler and three of his men rode up. He saw Anne Jason huddled under the cart with the smaller of her boys. The sight seemed to anger him.

"Jason, you'd better load that woman and kid in the cart and head for Fort Lodgepole."

Jason, beat out and wet to the skin, said: "You're orderin' me to leave the herd and. . . ."

"The herd will get there. If you're not at Deergrass to claim it, I'll tally every hoof and make settlement. Get her in the cart and drive her to Lodgepole."

"It ain't even my cart. It belongs to Rio."

Rio Reavley shambled up. He was about to tangle with Mixler on the point, but he could tell by the tone of Jason's voice how desperately he wanted to leave. His eyes traveled to the woman, and he said: "All right. Take the cart. I'll shack up with Wolf. I'll look after your cows, Dave."

Pecos learned of their departure eighteen hours later, when he returned with word that a Sioux war party had been following the herd, keeping watch of it from the flanks of the Black Hills. After making the report to Mixler and the Haltmans, he went to Reavley's camp and said: "I hear Jason and his family set out for the fort."

Reavley nodded. He was trying to boil coffee, but the sage-brush fuel was damp, and all he could get were great volumes of smoke. Standing by, watching him, were Geppert, Jardine, and Wolf Carson. They were a tired, ill-tempered crew.

Reavley said: "They took my wagon, what was left of it. We're down to pack horses."

"You shouldn't have let 'em. Not with war parties on the prowl."

"I guess maybe you don't like the way we're running our end of this outfit," Reavley said, getting to his feet.

"I'm not fighting with you. I'm on your side."

Reavley said: "Yeah." He looked into rainy darkness over west. "Damn it, I didn't want to see 'em go, but if you'd seen his old lady squattin' there under the cart. . . ."

"Trail herd's no place for woman," Wolf Carson said.

"She'd have made it all right," Reavley returned, "and maybe Callie would have, too, if Mixler'd taken the main trail up through the forks of the Powder. He wanted to get rid of 'em, and he has. He's got rid of Tom Mace . . . he's got rid of McCrae . . . he's got rid of Jason. I reckon maybe he thinks I'm next. Or you, Pecos, so don't turn your back on Star Glynn or Kiowa Johnny."

"Ever think of cutting the herd and driving to Deadwood with us?"

"Ever think of having Star Glynn shoot you right in the guts?"

"Sometimes. Sometimes I thought of it being the other way around."

"You got yourself a reputation, Pecos, and that I won't deny. But you'll be going up against something a lot tougher than Rasmussen when you tackle Glynn. Or Ed Ward. Mixler's got gunmen stacked pretty deep, and you'll have to climb through all of 'em before you cut that herd for Deadwood."

From the dark came Hernandez's voice: "Has *señor* seen the Keed shoot? Perhaps if *señor* would look in the leetle black book of Hernandez and see there the debt of feefty thousand dollar, lost by me to the Keed in shooting debts alone. . . ."

Big Jim said: "I can't see what difference it makes to Mixler. What if we do drive to Deadwood? That way we won't be laying claim on any of that Montana grass he has such a hanker for."

"You don't understand," Reavley said. "The Deergrass was just thrown open from the Blackfoot treaty reserve. This herd will do a nice job of grabbing it all. Big outfits like the Diamond Bar and the Sixty-Nine won't get a foothold. Mixler and the Haltmans will be kings of the country, just like they were in Texas. What if a couple of us little ones do stick it out? They'll still be in a position to lord it over us. No, he's holding the herd together. He'll do it in spite of you. He'll do it in spite of hell. The man ain't human. He never quits. He won't quit on this. He'll take those Rocking A steers along, and you can take your choice whether he does it with you alive or with you dead."

The Kid laughed and took his hat off to shake water from the brim. "Why, now, I'd rather he'd do it with me alive. I sure would."

It cleared in the morning. The herd moved without dust. It was good to breathe and be alive. For the first time in days, Hernandez unwrapped his guitar from its slicker and sang. When the Pecos Kid rode up, he said: "Today we do not scout for the Sioux?"

"We're not far from the Belle Fourche." He pointed to a purplish valley in the remote distance, northwest. "Mixler'll never stop the herd. We'll have to start cutting our stuff now."

They worked easily all morning, cutting Rocking A steers from the bunch, drifting them to one side, bringing them in with the drag. In this manner, a third of Mace's herd had been bunched when Mixler learned of it and came at a gallop. With him were five men headed by Star Glynn.

Mixler brought his horse in with a mean twist of the bridle. Anger showed in the way he carried himself. He barked: "Who told you to start cutting the herd?"

Pecos answered: "If you'll notice those are all Rocking A steers."

"If you want your cattle cut out, you're to come to me. Your job's scouting for Indians."

The Kid found a burr in his horse's mane and thoughtfully

removed it. Without shifting his eyes, he could see Star Glynn edging to one side, his body low in the saddle, a hip-out position that brought the butt of his Colt within easy reach. Ed Ward had moved in the other direction, but unlike Star Glynn, so slack and casual, he stood in the stirrups and kept his elbows close against his body. He wondered which of them was the fastest—Glynn, Ward, or big Clay Mixler. Glynn perhaps. He had that slack look, almost like Hernandez. Those were the ones to look out for. They made everything seem casual. They drew with shrugging, hitching movements, their guns exploding on the top of a hand flip. He'd heard that Glynn had killed eleven men. Maybe he'd killed twice times eleven. He wasn't the kind who talked about such things. He didn't file notches in those mother-of-pearl stocks on his .45s.

Pecos still picked at the cocklebur fragments. Hernandez and Jim Swing were riding up from the drag. He wondered if this would be the showdown. He wished Hernandez and Jim would stay back. It was too good a chance for Mixler, getting them all at once, out-gunned three to six.

The Kid tilted his head toward the blue summits of the mountains and drawled: "Them's the Black Hills, yonder. You recollect when we joined up we said they'd be the end of our trail."

"All right, make it the end of the trail. If you have a fancy for Deadwood, why don't you start out now?"

"Not without our cattle, seh."

Mixler was bent forward in his saddle, both hands on the pommel, a posture that accentuated the massive depth of his chest, the breadth of his shoulders. It placed his gun just back of his right hand.

"Not without your cattle? That's up to me. Everything's up to me. I'm running the herd. I'll run it as I see fit."

Hernandez heard him as he came to a stop. He cried: "You mean to take our cattle away from us and drive them to Montana? You mean you will fatten them on the Deergrass, and ship them by steamboat perhaps to Saint Louis, and . . . ?"

"Butch!" Pecos cut him off. Hernandez would go too far. It was playing into Mixler's hands. The showdown would come, but it would have to come later. It would have to come at a time and place chosen not by Mixler, but by himself. He saw Glynn move his horse a trifle, and shifted to match it, keeping Mixler between them.

Mixler shouted to Hernandez: "Whatever you got on your mind, say it right out. This is as good a place to settle it as any."

Pecos said softly: "We just want our cows. Tom Mace wanted 'em taken through to Deadwood, and that's what we aim to do. That was the understanding. You never said it was unreasonable before."

"We're behind schedule. We should have crossed the Belle Fourche last week. I can't let you hold up the herd while you do your cutting."

The Kid laughed and shrugged his shoulders. "If that's the way it is, why, I guess that's the way it is." He lifted his hand in the Confederate cavalryman's salute. "We await your orders, seh."

"Keep track of those Indians! Those are my orders. *We'll* worry about getting your stock cut out."

# IX

# " 'CUT YOUR OWN DAMNED STEERS!' "

Hernandez cursed steadily under his breath as they drifted toward the bench country. Finally he reined around and cried: "Was thees the Pecos Kid of old I heard, making wrinkles in his belly, bowing before that king of the gunman? Was thees the Pecos Keed that shot Querno and Alderdice, weeth two shots . . . *bang bang!* . . . in the hot dust of Guadalupe? Have you been eating so long the meat of the jack rabbit that your heart flutters like an old squaw at the thought of guns and powder smoke? My cheeks burn with shame that I should steek my tail between my legs and follow you the wrong way from six men weeth notches in their guns!"

Pecos said: "You like to be buried here?"

"I weel not be buried here, on thees prairie, even though he should throw three times six guns against me. Was it not told to me by a Gypsy in Tres Castillos that I would die reech and respected, amid the broad acres of my *hacienda*, to the music of my weeping *peones* and grandchildren, both by the hundreds, in bed, with my boots off, with gold in my pocket and all my debts paid up? Then how could I do anything but shoot thees *gringo* peeg before he could cock the hammer of his gun?"

"You're pretty good with that gun, Butch. But while we were getting three of them, they'd have gotten three of us. That'd still leave them in the majority. But nothing happened, and we're alive. *Alive* is a pretty good way to be."

"You will then let heem take the herd? There is no fortune

191

for us, waiting in Deadwood?"

"I didn't say that. It's just that we won't be able to do it alone. We'll need Reavley and Carson and all the men they can round up."

Pecos lay in his blankets. The herd was bedded down. Men on the night watch sang endlessly, riding the big circle. He could hear Jim, snoring on one side of him. Hernandez lay silently on the other.

He said: "Butch, are you awake?"

"*Sí*. Awake thees long time, thinking. We should not worry about cutting the Rocking A cattle, Keed. When the time comes, we will take our share, nine hundred or more, and drive toward Deadwood. Who cares for the brand? Is not a longhorn a longhorn? What could he prove once they were beefsteak in the bellies of twelve thousand miners?"

"I been thinking the same thing. We'll talk it over with Reavley."

Pecos nudged Big Jim and said: "Get up!"

"Mornin' already?" Jim muttered.

"We were going to see Reavley, remember?"

The horse wrangler was taking a nap with a blanket up over his head. He woke up when his remuda started running in a circle and said: "Wait, damn it, before they bust that string corral down and run clear to the Black Hills." He saw who it was. "Oh, you boys taking a turn at night herd?"

Pecos said: "Injuns."

The wrangler looked scared and roped out the horses for them.

Reavley's camp was about two miles away. Only old Pancake Jeffers was there. He sat up with a heavy Sharps rifle in his hands. "Oh," he said, "it's you."

"Where's Rio?" Pecos asked.

"He ain't here." Pancake couldn't get over his suspicion of them because they stayed at Mixler's camp.

"I can see that. Where is he?"

"Well, I guess he's yonder in the dry wash, but, if you go walking up on him after dark, you're asking for a Forty-Four slug in the belly."

Hernandez said: "Perhaps we, too, should be sleeping in the dry wash."

Big Jim said: "*Now* who's making the jack rabbit talk?"

"*Señor*, you are talking to Hernandez Pedro Gonzales, son of the Fuente, son of the Flanagan. Among my ancestors were the noblemen of the. . . ."

The Kid said: "You're a shanty Irishman and a greaser, and you'd have been in your grave two years ago with that Medanos rope around your neck if I hadn't ridden twenty miles with the *caballería*."

"What is the point of thees?"

"The point is you're making too much noise, and one of these days I won't be able to save your neck."

Pecos raised his hand in a signal for the others to stay back. He rode alone to the edge of the dry wash. There he pulled up and called softly: "Rio!"

Reavley answered almost instantly. "Yeah! Who is it?"

"Pecos. Jim and Hernandez are with me."

"Oh." Pecos heard the double click of metal as he lowered the hammer of his gun. "All right, come down."

"You're a light sleeper."

"It pays a man sometimes."

Hernandez said: "You theenk that lobo, Mixler, would really try bushwhack?"

"I don't think one way or the other. I just don't take any chances I don't have to."

The Kid said: "You better come with us, Rio."

"Where are you going?"

"Deadwood."

"Tonight?"

"No, not tonight. We're supposed to turn at the Belle Fourche. We decided to make the break earlier. About four days from now, when we reach that big dry bottom they call the Ironrod."

Wolf Carson, sneaking down the dry wash with his rifle up, asked: "What's that you're saying?"

Reavley said: "The boys want us to string along with 'em to Deadwood." He stood, gangling and leather-tough, thinking about it. "Oh, hell. It'd take two, three days to cut our stuff out of the herd. Mixler'd never stand for it. He's got us too far out-gunned."

"A steer's a steer."

"You mean just cut a chunk out of the herd and drive 'em? You might get into a heap of trouble trying to sell the other man's brand."

"Not in Deadwood. Anything goes in Deadwood."

While Reavley was thinking, Wolf Carson said: "Well, by grab, I'm in with you. I only got a handful of stock, but I'm in with you. I'd rather make one big gamble than live under the heel of that timber wolf for another thousand miles to Montana."

"All right." They were hard words for Reavley to say. He'd set his mind on getting a piece of the Deergrass, but the departure of Carson and Pecos would have left him alone at Mixler's mercy. "How do you plan to do it? Our cut will be about three thousand. . . ."

"Thirty-six hundred. I promised McCrae."

"Thirty-six hundred, then. Will we just cut them off the drag?"

"No, I'm not taking the drag. We got to have cattle willing

to travel, because we'll have to run 'em all night through that Injun country. I noticed every morning that there's one bunch always hits out together. When the time comes, we'll cut them loose and run 'em up the bottoms. I haven't planned beyond that. No way of planning . . . we don't know what Mixler'll do."

Wolf Carson giggled and did a polka step in his patched-up boots. "Sweet name o' hell! That'll be just like twisting a grizzly's tail."

Reavley said: "He'll have us out-gunned."

"And we'll have him by surprise. We might be half a day's travel off before he notices. Those cowboys, eating dirt off the swing and the drag, won't pay attention. The wagons will be four miles ahead. Star Glynn and his gunmen drift off somewhere every day and sleep in the shade till the cook wagon catches up with them. If we play it right, he won't get a fight organized until nightfall."

"And what then?"

"I know that country, yonder. So does Big Jim. There's a blind cañon back in the foothills where we'll be able to hold them off for a week. How many men can you round up?"

"Jardine and Pancake. Maybe Al Geppert. With us, that makes eight."

Big Jim murmured: "Eight against thirty."

"They won't all of 'em be after us. This is Sioux country. Mixler won't take too big a chance on scattering the herd. Besides, there's a couple more I can pick up. Hank Wellens might go, and that horse wrangler. He's been having trouble with Mixler."

Hernandez said: "My countryman, Gonzales, already love me like a brother. Besides, I owe heem the sum of one hundred *pesos*, and how will he collect unless he come along to Deadwood?"

195

They talked details for an hour, and returned to their blankets. At grub pile in the morning, Pecos noticed Star Glynn intently watching him. For just an instant it gave him a nervous, gutless feeling. It was almost as though he were a kid again, instead of twenty-eight with half a hundred gunfights under his belt. Only you never get over the fear of dying. And you never quite get over your fear of a man like Star Glynn. He wondered, if the chips were down and they faced each other, which would win. He shrugged it off, wiped out his plate with a handful of grass, and tossed it in the plunder box. They'd never face each other that way. Not while Star had Ed Ward, Kiowa Johnny, and Billy Six-Spot at his back.

After grub pile, Pecos rode with Big Jim up rising country. They turned with the sunrise warm on their backs to watch the herd.

"Where's Hernandez?" Pecos asked.

"Yonder," he tilted his head toward the hills. "He's singing those damned love songs again, making a lot of fool talk about how the women will follow him around Deadwood. He's going to get in trouble, Kid. He's going to get killed. That Deadwood's a tough town."

"So was Maverly a tough town. And Denver, and Cheyenne, and Dodge. Hernandez isn't buried in any of them towns."

"He would be if it hadn't been for us. Damn it all, maybe we're making a mistake. Maybe we ought to take these dogies right through to Deergrass. We'd be big ranchers up there, Pecos! We'd grow with the country."

Pecos had been thinking along those lines himself, but again he dismissed it from his mind. "It's no use, Jim. They're Mace's steers. Half of 'em. And Mace wanted 'em driven to Deadwood."

# X

# "THE BIG STAMPEDE"

Big Jim had always dreamed of owning a ranch of his own. That
night, lying by the fire, he got out a battered volume entitled
HOW TO MAKE ONE HUNDRED THOUSAND
DOLLARS IN THE CATTLE BUSINESS OUT WEST and
said: "Listen to what this book says, Butch. If you really want to
pay off your debts, you'll do it a hell of a lot easier trailing to the
Deergrass than to Deadwood, and this book proves it."

Hernandez was dreamy-eyed, plucking his guitar. "In
Deadwood you sell the steer for feefty, maybe one hundred
dollars the head. In Deergrass for ten, maybe fifteen dollars
the head. Your book says drive to Deergrass? . . . then I say
throw your book away, for it is a fool."

Big Jim cried: "Wait! The author takes care of that on page
twelve. Quit playing that guitar and listen here."

While Big Jim was reading, the Kid stood, and moved back
from the firelight. A candle was burning inside Haltman's
Conestoga, and he could see the shadow movements of men
against the cloth top. One was Mixler, another Vern
Haltman. There was a third shadow he imagined to be Ed
Ward, but he couldn't be sure in silhouette.

Mixler was talking; he could tell that by the jerking movements of his head, emphasizing the words. They were having
a big powwow. A man could hear easily through the canvas
wagon sheets, he was thinking. It was a temptation, but he
gave it up. They'd have sentries out. Rasmussen, Kiowa

197

Johnny—either would like the chance to put a bullet or a knife in his back.

Big Jim was reading, squinting to make out the words by firelight: " . . . and beware the buyer who offers to buy stock for double or triple the market price, for he is most certainly a charlatan."

Hernandez, still softly strumming the guitar, said dreamily: "One time I knew a man from Charley Town. He was a stage driver. He was not so bad." A smile touched his lips. "He had a wife. She was not so bad, either. Oh, a little fat maybe, but what is wrong weeth that?"

The Kid, still watching the covered wagon, said: "How old was she?"

"So she was a little bit old. What is wrong weeth *that?*"

"Was she good-looking?"

"No, she was not so good-looking. She had big jowls, and there was a mole on the side of her mouth, and she dyed her hair red, I theenk, but what is wrong with that?" He put his guitar down. "Why should you laugh at thees poor old woman with her red face and her big nose? Weeth her husband gone, driving the stage for two, three days at a time and never home? You should come from Chihuahua and have respect for women. Besides, she made good apple pie."

"Oh, hell!" said Big Jim, and put the book down.

The Kid could no longer see Mixler's shadow. He'd moved away from the light. The camp was quieting down. There were the night sounds of cattle. A cowboy somewhere sang the interminable verses of "The Rabble Soldier."

Hernandez wrapped his guitar in the slicker, yawned, and said: "Time for sleeping, Keed. It will be a long tomorrow."

Pecos lay awake, looking at the stars. It had been dry for the last few days, with a scent of smoke from forest fires in the

Black Hills. The slight veil of smoke magnified the stars, making them appear to be suspended scarcely a pistol shot overhead. The night herder, to the slow rhythm of his horses' hoofs, was singing.

> **I cry for rye whiskey**
> **Wherever I roam.**
> **I'm an old rabble soldier**
> **And Dixie's my home.**

Pecos had avoided Reavley all day. He didn't want to be seen talking to him. Mixler was no fool. He was wary as a wolf. He'd be quick to suspect. Now, with the camp asleep, he was tempted to hunt out Reavley's bed and talk to him. There were some details to be arranged.

He rolled to his side. The candle was no longer burning in Haltman's Conestoga. Through the wheels of the cook wagon he could see the dull glow of coals where the coffee sat, keeping hot for the night herders.

The cowboy's dreary chant, after coming close, had receded, but because he knew the words so well, he could still understand them.

> **Oh bring me cold lager**
> **And scrape off the foam.**
> **I'm an old rabble soldier**
> **And Dixie's my home.**

He dozed and came suddenly awake. He restrained the impulse to get up. He lay full length in his blankets. It had been a sound, a movement. He wasn't sure. Hernandez was sleeping, and farther off he could hear the regular snoring of Big Jim Swing.

He listened as minutes went by. Now, even the cowboy's singing had been engulfed by the vast prairie night. An ember in the fire popped and showered coals in the air. It was a slight thing, but after the long silence it hit him like a gunshot.

He sat up. His hand closed on the butt of his six-shooter. Then he saw movement, a shadow between him and the cook wagon, and he knew who it was. Lita Haltman.

He was clothed, aside from his boots. He pulled the boots on, strapped his gun around his waist. Then he spoke her name, and she came toward him.

"Pecos."

"Yes."

She was frightened. As she came close, he could see the rapid rise and fall of her breast. Her lips were parted slightly. Her eyes kept searching the darkness around.

He said: "It's just Hernandez and Jim."

She reached, and he took hold of her arm. He was surprised how slim and small her hand was. A man forgets about women, living whole months and years in a rough land of men.

"Pecos," she whispered, "you can't stay any longer. You can't, Pecos. You have to get out. Tonight."

"You heard what Mixler was cooking up at that meeting?"

"They found something out about you. Something you're going to do. I don't know what it was. You went somewhere last night, and Kiowa Johnny followed you. You went to see Reavley, I know that much."

Pecos cursed through his teeth. He should have known Mixler'd have the 'breed watching him, checking on him.

She said: "Pecos, they'll try to kill you."

She stood very close, looking up at him. Her hands clutched the front of his shirt. He could smell her hair. It had a fresh wind and sage odor. He had an impression of her lithe body under the clothes she wore, and for a moment he forgot danger and everything, except that she was there.

"I have to go," she whispered.

He hadn't noticed—he had hold of her arms.

"Pecos," she whispered, "they mustn't find me here."

"*Who* find you here?"

"You know!"

She sounded as if she was going to cry. He thought she meant Mixler. She was afraid to have Mixler find them together because Mixler would be jealous. The thought made him go hot and cold. His hands closed down on her arms, just below her shoulders. She twisted from side to side, but he didn't let her go. He said: "You don't care anything for Mixler."

She didn't answer.

He shook her back and forth, harder than he intended. Her hair came down and fell around her shoulders. "Answer me . . . you don't care anything about him. He has a wife back in Texas. He has a son as old as you . . . don't you know that?"

"Yes," she whispered. "I don't care anything for him. I hate him. Do you hear, I hate him!"

He stopped. He felt ashamed. He let her go. "I'm sorry."

"Why did you talk that way?"

"I'm sorry," he repeated.

He was thinking that, if he went to Deadwood, it would mean leaving her behind. He didn't want to leave her with Mixler. Not even though three of her brothers were along. She pulled away from him.

"Lita," he said, "wait a minute!"

"I can't stay," she whispered.

He noticed for the first time that she was barefooted. She ran with long steps, with the lithe grace of a prairie animal.

He stood for several seconds after she was out of sight

around the Haltman wagon. His own danger asserted itself again. It occurred to him that, if Kiowa had been watching last night, he'd be watching again tonight. He'd have seen her. He'd carry the news straight to Mixler.

He walked to the shadow of the cook wagon. There he stopped, listened. No sound. Just the slight snapping of the fire, the thud of coffee in the big pot. He could see Haltman's wagon, with men sleeping under it. There was a tent beyond where Mixler slept. Farther off, horses moved restlessly in the night wrangler's rope corral. The herd was a mile off, bedded down on a grassy slope.

He heard the soft hoof-thud as a rider came up out of the darkness and dismounted by the fire. It was a young cowboy who went by the name of Rawhide. The cowboy poured a cup of coffee and was hunkered back on his heels, blowing on it, when he noticed the Pecos Kid standing, watching him.

"Hello, Rawhide," the Kid said.

After a start of surprise, the cowboy laughed. "Want a cup of coffee? It's thick and black as N'Orleans sorghum."

"Thanks."

He waited for the cowboy, brightly revealed by the glow of the fire, to pour one for him. The cowboy held the cup out. He had to step out from the wagon to take it.

The Pecos Kid knew the danger it would place him in. His fingers touched the butt of his Colt, making certain it rode in the right place. His eyes searched the darkness for the last time. He stepped forward, reaching for the cup, but at the final instant, as firelight struck him, he pivoted away.

The cup fell, struck the ground, and lashed hot liquid across his boots. Someone had moved from the shadow of an empty barrel that had been lifted down from Haltman's wagon. A gun flashed. Explosion split the night stillness.

Pecos felt the whip of the bullet, passing within inches of

his shoulder. His own gun was in his hand. The pivot had ended in a crouch by the front wheel. He fired twice, fast as he could thumb the hammer. Instinct told him the first shot connected.

He saw a man reel forward into the starlight, a tall man, limber-legged, gun dangling in his hand. He stumbled and fell forward with his head bent under him. The man was Ed Ward.

Pecos started to get up, one hand gripping the wagon spokes. Then gunfire came at him from two directions. The cowboy's horse, frightened, started away, dragging his bridle. The new burst of gunfire turned him. He galloped toward the cook wagon. The Pecos Kid rammed his gun away and, diving forward, got hold of the bridle.

Bullets tore the sod under him. The horse sunfished and started to run. Pecos got hold of a stirrup. He was being dragged. His legs were under the horse's belly. Hoofs beat him across the thigh. For the space of two or three seconds all he could do was hold tight, then with a desperate effort he grabbed the horn, pulled himself to the saddle.

Fifty or sixty yards of darkness now separated him from the cook fire. They were still shooting, but none of the bullets was close. He still had his Colt, and Rawhide's carbine was in a saddle scabbard. He got the broncho stopped. He poked empty cartridge cases from the Colt, and reloaded from his belt.

Hernandez shouted his name. He answered through cupped hands. He sat with his gun poised, not knowing friend from enemy in the dark. Then the shooting diminished, and there was another sound, a rumble, like distant thunder, earth-shaking.

From far away came a cowboy's warning shout: "Stampede!"

The herd was in movement. By moonlight, Pecos could see dust, a silvery cloud, and through it the shine of horns, the dark backs of cattle. They seemed to be in flux, like the sea. Men forgot the fight. They were at the rope corrals, trying to catch their mounts. Content with a bridle or hackamore, they mounted bareback.

Now the thunder was growing. Baffled by echo and darkness, the herd was coming that way. Pecos thought of the girl. He spurred toward the wagon. His horse veered from the fallen body of Ed Ward. He called: "Lita!" She answered him from off in the dark. She was riding at an angle from the herd.

"Keed!" It was Hernandez, with a gun still in his hand. He ran up, got hold of his stirrup. His teeth flashed white against his dark skin. "They are coming, Keed! Perhaps they weel run all the way to Deadwood, no?"

"Where's Jim?" Then he saw the big fellow running up with a war sack under one arm, a Winchester, Colt, and cartridge belt under the other.

"What a hell of a night to start a ruckus," he said. His high-pitched, accusing voice sounded out of place against the rising thunder of the herd. "We got to get out of here, Kid. We got to ride that horse double."

Hernandez jeered: "Triple we weel ride heem! What do you theenk he is, one horse or an elephant?"

It could now be seen that the main body of the herd was swinging slightly to the northeast, but still the later wash of it would most certainly engulf the camp. From down the knoll riders were on the gallop, firing, trying to mill the leaders.

Hernandez was now down behind a wagon wheel, gun poised. "Ride and save yourself, Keed!" he said over his shoulder.

"The hell with you. We have a quarter minute. Get the saddles over here."

Pecos tied the broncho to the wagon, waited with his gun drawn. Big Jim was beside him.

"You think they'll turn 'em?" Jim asked.

"We won't turn 'em, but we might split 'em if they don't stack up too deep."

They waited a quarter minute as the herd roared ever closer. A portion had split off and gone past to the east. Its dust rolled in a thick blanket, making it hard to breathe. They saw the first steers veering off from the wagons. Then others closed in, a dense, wall-eyed, terrified mass.

The Kid picked a steer and fired. It went down, digging its head, with its hindquarters rolling high. He heard the crash of guns on both sides of him. There were cattle going down and cattle piling over them, plunging, getting up again.

Two steers came on, directly toward the wagon. One was shot and fell only a dozen yards away; the other ran straight on and crashed the wagon box. Bawling, the animal got to its feet, ran, and was carried away by the mass flowing to the south.

No longer able to see the herd, they fired blindly. The flames of their guns looked ruddy through air too thick to breathe. Only the bawl of crippled cattle, the settling layers of dust, the guns hot in their hands.

"We are still here," said Hernandez. "We still live . . . we still breathe. Did I not say I would die reech and respected in the midst of my acres and my grandchildren in Chihuahua?"

The Kid said: "Wait here. I'll ride and see if I can find the remuda. I think they headed southeast."

He galloped the broncho, digging dirt from his eyes and nostrils. Somehow he'd been cut across both lips. He had no memory of anything striking him. Dust clouds were clearing now, and he could see.

The cattle were far away and still running. They'd split

into sections. After a mile, he saw two riders—Wolf Carson and Geppert.

"Where's Rio?" he asked.

"Yonder." Wolf jerked his head toward upcountry. "You want us to bring him?"

"Tell him one end of that herd took out in the direction of Deadwood. It'll be our last chance. We better keep 'em going."

The remuda had been scattered, but it hadn't run far. He gathered a dozen horses and herded them back.

Hernandez plodded up from the darkness, moaning: "My guitar . . . my guitar . . . it is gone. Why did I not bring it weeth me instead of thees old apple-horn saddle? Why did I leave it, my sweetheart, to die under the hoofs of that herd?"

"We'll buy one in Deadwood. Rope yourself a horse. I don't know how long I can hold 'em."

# XI

# "SITTING BULL'S LAND"

Eastward they found cattle scattered for miles. All fear run out of them, they were grazing in jack timber and brush-filled draws. They gathered them in bunches of forty or fifty and kept crowding them into a big dry wash that slanted back toward the hills. After a couple of hours, they met Rio Reavley and his men, working ridges up from the south.

Brought together, Pecos made a rough tally. "Thirty-one hundred," he said. "If we get twenty-five hundred of them to Deadwood, I won't complain."

With Reavley and Carson were Pancake, Al Geppert, and Fred Jardine. That made a total of eight. Gonzales and the wrangler would probably come, but there was scant chance of finding them. They drove on with what men and horses they had, up miles of dry wash, as the sides steepened and jackpine commenced to lay black blankets over the hillsides.

The dry wash forked, and forked again as it cut into the steeper hills. They drove the herd across slide rock and knee-high bramble to a bench terrace, running for miles north and south, fronting the first great ridge of the Black Hills.

Dawn, in streaks of pink and yellow, silhouetted the summits. Dust still hovered in a fine cloud below, dust that first looked like gray fog and then turned the color of corn meal as the sun struck it.

"See them?" Hernandez asked, coming to a stop beside Pecos.

"The herd? Yes, it's 'way yonder. No, *'way* over. We come farther than we thought. Either that or the main bunch made a half circle and run over west. Must be ten miles off."

After long watching, they could tell that cowboys were at work, gathering the herd. It would be a big job. Mixler would have the tough choice of letting this thirty-one hundred go to Deadwood, or letting the main herd graze and scatter, and probably end up in one of Sitting Bull's stew pots.

"Better get moving," Pecos said.

The drive went on all day, along the bench, across a vast mountain shoulder, and finally down through rock and pine to the depths of Ironrod Coulée. A stream flowed in the bottom, clear and cold. In its deep riffles, one could see the darting, grayish shapes of fingerling trout. It was mining country, prospected before Sitting Bull left the agency, and placer pits had been sunk here and there in the bench ground.

"We'll camp now," Pecos said.

Darkness settled more rapidly here than on the plains. They risked building a little fire, and put it out as soon as they'd finished making coffee and doughgod.

The herd spread out, grazing through the lush grass. High in the rocks a coyote howled.

Rio stood up, and in the darkness they could hear him fooling with his Winchester.

"There'll be trouble tonight," he said.

"I doubt it." Pecos sounded sleepy. He lay on his back with clasped hands under his head, looking at the stars. "He'll wait . . . Mixler will. He don't go around just shooting off powder for the hell of it. He'll see where we're going, then he'll go ahead and lay a nice, cross-fire ambush, by *good strong daylight* so's those gunmen can get us in the fine notch of their sights."

"Just the same, I'm watching the rocks."

"Sure. We'll split the night in half. That all right?"

Reavley awakened him about midnight. Pecos sat up, got his boots on, and stamped life into the cold leather. Hernandez, hearing him, also got up, but Big Jim still snored.

"See anything?" Pecos asked.

Reavley gestured, but it was vague in the dark. "Yes. There was somebody yonder. Came sneaking along. I followed. Tried to get a look at him, but that timber is blacker than a suit of spades."

"Injun?"

"It was a white man. He doubled back, and I saw him a quarter mile off, getting on his horse. He didn't get on the offside like an Injun. I had a hunch it was Evas Williams."

Hernandez asked: "Should I wake Beeg Jeem?"

Pecos said: "Let him sleep. He ate the drag on this herd all day. He earned it."

The night was quiet. Pecos and Hernandez scouted opposite rims of the valley, saw nothing. The camp was already awake, when they came down through the gray light of dawn.

Cattle were balky, and it took hours of hard riding to get them in steady movement, across meadow, through brush, through rocky narrows. Night had left a chill in the valley, then suddenly a bright sun drove it away, and the morning was hot. Sunlight reflected from cliffs and talus rock. Pecos's shirt was wet. It stuck to his back. Riding, shouting, swinging the rope goad had made him forget the danger of ambush. He remembered it now, and turned his horse up a deer trail that zigzagged through rock and timber to the north rim.

High above the valley floor, he stopped to let his horse breathe. The air was clear and dry, filled with the slightly burned odor of summer-dry pine. Mountain summits covered with forest rose to the east. At one place he could see a switchback trail terminating at a series of chalky-looking scars. Those were dumps extending downhill from the mouths of tunnels where some wandering prospector had taken his chance on Indians while exploring the outcrop of a gold quartz vein.

A rider slowly climbed the far side. It was too far to tell for sure, but Pecos decided it was Hernandez.

Pecos kept riding, following a contour of the mountain. Hernandez had disappeared in a rocky draw. Pecos saw him again much later, miles farther, approaching another summit.

Pecos dismounted and bunkered in the cover of trees. By slow degrees, his eyes swept the vast country beneath him. From a distance, when the wind was right, he could hear the bawling of cattle. At other times there were only the cries of veering eagles, the vast sigh of wind currents through evergreens.

He was hungry. He closed his eyes to rest them. He dozed for a few seconds and, on opening his eyes, glimpsed movement far across the valley. A man was on foot, tiny from distance, climbing. It wasn't Hernandez. Hernandez had long before reached a higher level. Then he glimpsed a second man, perhaps a quarter mile to the west, just disappearing in timber.

He waited, but he didn't reappear. Now the first man was gone from sight, too. Suddenly he realized that Hernandez was coming from above, horseback, following a twisting trail where talus rock sloped from the face of a cliff, and the men were below, under cover, waiting for him.

He cupped his hands and shouted. Hernandez did not look up. He shouted again and again, but Hernandez remained bent forward in his saddle, eyes on the treacherous descent. Pecos drew his six-shooter, and, moving to a reflecting surface of rock, he fired.

Hernandez still rode as the echoes pounded away. Then, after what seemed to be a long wait, he jerked erect and looked. It had taken him that long for the sound to reach him.

Pecos whipped off his shirt and started to signal with it. A second later, Hernandez twisted from the saddle, drawing his Winchester as he went, and dropped to all fours.

He fired. A spurt of gunsmoke appeared, hung suspended on the air. Instantly there were gunsmokes down the mountainside. Then the *crack-crack* of rifle fire came to Pecos. It was furious for a while, then it tapered off with groups of shots separated by intervals of silence.

Hernandez was on his stomach, working his way from one rock cover to the next. Pecos could see him, although he was hidden from his attackers down the slope.

Pecos mounted and picked his way downhill. In timber, he had only brief glimpses of the battle across from him. He could no longer tell where Hernandez was, although the brittle cracking of gunfire still came, each shot multiplied by echoes that chased it like rapid handclaps.

He was nearing the bottom. A bullet stung the rocks five or six feet to his right and whined off with a vicious discord. He should have expected it, but it had come as a surprise. His movement was pure reflex. He spurred, doubled over, his body behind the horse, his rifle in his hands, as more bullets whined around him.

Jackpine ripped at him, hid him from view. He dismounted. There was a rock reef now separating him from his attackers. He clambered on hands and feet, reached the sharp-broken crest, fell face down in needle-sharp juniper.

He found himself looking down on a tiny feeder gulch. A haze of gunsmoke had ascended and drifted languidly on the hot air. There was movement below and to the right. A man was crawling on all fours. Pecos aimed and fired with one movement, and saw the grayish shower of dirt as his bullet tore under him. He took coarser sight, fired again, again, fast as his hand could operate the lever of the rifle.

Other guns opened up. Bullets were coming from two directions. He'd stumbled on the main ambush. He slid boots first back down the reef, found his horse, rode around the slope staying in timber, and came out with a view of the bottoms.

The herd was half a mile away. Only the lead steers were in view. Jardine and Reavley had stopped them. Reavley heard the crash and clatter of Pecos's descent and started to lift his gun.

"Me! Pecos!"

Reavley waited, watching, and made sure. Then he started up the valley at a gallop. A gun exploded from high among the rocks. Reavley was hit. The bullet went through him and pounded gray dust from the earth beyond. Reavley stayed with his horse for a second, and then fell, sprawled face up on the ground.

The ambusher fired again, aiming at Jardine. Jardine had whirled his horse around. The horse reared, and that saved him.

Pecos, on a low shoulder of bank, turned and saw the man hunkered, leveling a third cartridge into his rifle. Even at two hundred and fifty yards he could tell who it was. Star Glynn.

Pecos had no time to aim. He took a snap shot, and the bullet, showering Star Glynn with dirt, made him miss Jardine.

Pecos cursed through his teeth. Firing uphill, he'd made the most elementary of mistakes and shot too low. He fired again, but Glynn was already lunging on his side to the cover of some fallen timber nearby.

Pecos turned, rode on a slanting course uphill, through timber. When steepness made the horse lose footing, he sprang off and climbed. He stopped with his lungs splitting for air. For a second he was dizzy. He lay with one cheek pressed against a sun-hot piece of slide rock while he got his breath. Then he sat up and recovered his bearings.

He could see the heap of logs where Glynn had placed himself, but now he was gone. The herd was all under his gaze. Lead steers, frightened by gunfire, had turned back. Meeting the press of the herd, they were jam-packed and milling, horns tossed high.

Reavley hadn't moved. He lay face down. The sun raised a metallic gleam from the receiver of his rifle, which had fallen in low buckbush. Big Jim was riding on the far side of the herd, squeezed against the cañon wall. Pecos shouted to him. Bawling of the herd covered his voice. Back on the drag was Pancake and Al Geppert. He couldn't see Wolf Carson.

He heard his name called, looked across, saw Hernandez riding downhill. *All clear,* Hernandez was signaling to him.

Pecos met him in the bottom. "They bushwhacked Reavley . . . did you happen to notice that?"

"I notice," Hernandez whispered through his teeth. "It was Star Glynn. Someday I theenk I will kill heem. You hear? That is a promise. Someday I will kill heem."

# XII

## "WILDFIRE"

They buried Reavley in a shallow grave and heaped rocks over it. Then they went on, along an ever-steepening valley. At night they pocketed the herd and gathered, a lean-faced, silent group, around a tiny cook fire hidden between the steep banks of a gully. They drank coffee, and gnawed jerked beef that was tough as the sole of a moccasin.

"Last of the jerky," Pancake said. "We'll have a doughgod tomorrow. I don't know what'n hell we'll do after that."

"Plenty of beef," Jim said in his treble. "And you won't be able to tell *that* beef from jerky, either, if we run 'em much farther. I hope them Deadwood miners haven't got their mouths set for a rare, tender steak, because they'll need teeth like a winter wolf to chaw these critters."

Pecos said: "After eating pack rat for the last year, they won't complain if their beef's got a little substance to it. Those miners will sit down to our steaks and think they come from Delmonico's back in Noo Yawk."

Geppert said: "If we can get 'em there."

"We'll get 'em there."

There was no alarm during the night, none the next day. Hernandez, scouting for trail, rode far ahead and returned at sundown with word that they would soon reach some elevated park lands and, after a few miles of those, could cross a rocky escarpment and drop down on the headwaters of the Spearfish. This in turn would take them north to the

Redwater, and, following that south again, they would reach Deadwood.

Pecos asked: "How long will it take us?"

"To the Spearfish? I theenk two days. Maybe we run these cow like hell we make it tomorrow."

"Then let's run 'em like hell."

Pecos, Carson, and Big Jim took the early watch. They returned about midnight, and Geppert, Hernandez, and Jardine took over. Old Pancake, who was stove up from rheumatism, cared for the remuda.

It seemed to Pecos he'd barely crawled in his blankets when he awoke with the raw feel of smoke in his throat. The stars were hazy. As he stood, he heard the crash of running feet. Hernandez shouted: "Fire! Forest fire. She's ahead, running thees way. Where the hell? I can see notheeng! Where are you?"

Pecos answered him. The camp was up. Horses for morning were on picket ropes, saddled, ready. In a matter of seconds, every man was mounted.

Geppert and Jardine quickly followed Hernandez into camp.

Pancake said: "We better get the hobbles off these bronc's. If that herd starts to move, they'll tromp 'em to mincemeat."

Pecos said: "Men, grab yourselves an extra horse. Get him on a lead string before they drift back to Texas."

The herd was up, bawling, milling around. The stars, visible only a minute before, had been covered by blowing layers of smoke. It made a dense, thick darkness. A man could scarcely see the ears of the horse he was riding.

Geppert shouted: "I got my horse fixed to lead. What in hell are we waiting for?"

"Hold on!" Pecos stopped them a second. "We'll head

downvalley. We'll stop at the forks. If the herd runs, we'll try to mill 'em there. These fires run in streaks. If it goes down the main channel, we'll head up the south gulch."

They rode, trusting the instincts of their horses, down the valley. Smoke, ever more dense, made a man's eyes water, his lungs raw. A horse stumbled and fell. Pecos could hear Hernandez, cursing in Spanish. He stopped. "You all right, Butch?"

"My horse is lame."

"Can he travel?"

"We will see."

The others were ahead of them. Pecos waited for ten seconds that seemed like a minute. He could see the fire, a brownish red line, through smoke and flame that slanted down the mountainside. It ran before the wind, was carried by heat-draught into the narrow V of the cañon. He drew his silk kerchief, rode until his horse splashed the creek, and bent over, dipped it, squeezed it out, and breathed through it.

"Keed!" Hernandez said.

"Here I am."

Hernandez was bareback on his spare horse. They rode on, a steady trot and gallop, taking their chances among rocks, windfalls, and prospect holes. The wind seemed stronger now. It blew smoke in dense layers with once in a while a current of clear air that was refreshing as spring water on the desert. The cañon turned, and turned again. Suddenly they crashed deep in brush, and for a moment Pecos had no idea where they were.

"Pecos!" he heard Jim Swing shout from the gloom ahead of them.

He answered and rode, bent low over his horse, clawing brush out of his way. They descended steeply and climbed steeply. It was a dry feeder stream. Underfoot was grassy earth. The cañon walls seemed to be nowhere close. Pecos was baffled, turned around. Even the breeze seemed to have changed. He called Jim's name again, heard the answer from an unexpected direction, rode toward it.

Now he could see a little. Jim and the others were there, waiting.

Jim said: "I thought something'd happened to you. Where's Butch?"

"I am here, bareback, leading a lame horse. Where are *you?* Where are all of us?"

"This is the cañon forks."

Now that they'd stopped, Pecos could hear bawling as the herd moved behind them.

Wolf Carson said: "There won't be much left to deliver in Deadwood after they run through this hell hole."

Pecos said: "They're not running hard."

The cañon would contain them, rough ground keeping some of the animals moving against the current. You need plenty of room for a real stampede.

"Think we can turn 'em here?"

"We might if the smoke cleared a little."

They rode slowly across the bottoms. A cross-current of wind flowed down the gulch from the southeast, carrying smoke away. Here there was only a thin fog. They could see a rocky horizon on the south; downcañon the smoke lay in drifts against the north wall and veiled some narrows where rock walls closed in.

Jardine said: "We'll have to keep 'em here or they'll run to kingdom come."

Now they were close to the narrows. Jardine, who was in the lead, unexpectedly wheeled his horse and shouted. Gunfire spurted from two directions, and bullet shock cut the sound in his throat.

The slug knocked him sidewise from his horse. He fell, but the fall ended in a scramble toward cover, so Pecos, who was behind, knew there was life left in him. Pecos spurred straight forward, bent, and tried to lift the man up beside him. Jardine, while tall and slim, was heavier than Pecos expected.

They were caught in a crossfire. A slug tore between the horse's legs, cut a furrow under Jardine's lifted shoulders. Pecos felt the sting of pellets, the wind whip of lead. His horse lunged in a circle. Pecos clung to Jardine, and Jardine to him. Then Jardine, shaking off bullet shock, made a wild grab, got the cantle, and dragged himself up till he lay behind the saddle.

It had taken about three seconds. The interval seemed timeless, something plucked out of space when a thousand thoughts exploded through a man's brain. Pecos expected the shock of a bullet, the blackness, with a ringing in his ears, but an instant later he was as certain that no bullet *could* touch him. He felt proof against them. He could have ridden through ten thousand hails of lead with none of them touching him. He carried with him a memory of their voices. Mixler's voice, Ellis Haltman's voice. He hadn't expected the Haltmans to take part in a bushwhack. But Ellis was a hothead. . . .

Hernandez, in the black haze somewhere, called his name.

"Get to going!" Pecos shouted back. He had a hard time getting his voice up with the raw smoke in his throat. "Get to going before the herd traps you."

Mixler had been waiting for that. He'd expected to cut all of them down at the narrows with pressure from the herd giving them no chance for escape. Only the herd, blinded and baffled, had moved too slowly.

Pecos kept riding. He still had the spare horse on a lead string. The steep rocks of the cañon stopped them. He turned and followed a contour. He found what seemed to be a trail.

It soon petered out, but the horse kept climbing despite slide rock that gave away underfoot, despite the double load on his back.

"Can you ride?" Pecos asked.

"I think so," Jardine grunted from the effort of speaking. "You take that other bronc'. But tie my feet down. One whole side of me feels dead."

"Where you hit?"

"Chest. High up some place."

Pecos dismounted, tied Jardine's boots in the stirrups, which he snubbed tight. Then, riding bareback with a rope hackamore, he went on, hunting a steep trail, climbing, always climbing. He heard hoofs somewhere back of him on the smoke-shrouded slope and thought without good reason that it was Hernandez.

"Butch?" he called.

There was a hesitation, then a voice: "Yes, Keed?"

It wasn't Hernandez. It was Kiowa Johnny, trying to sound like him. That sneaking, killing half-breed, Kiowa Johnny. There'd be others with him. He had to keep going, find safety, a place where he could get Jardine down and bandage him.

After long climbing, he heard Jardine say: "I'm bleeding, Pecos. You got to let me down."

He stopped. There was no moon or stars, but he was able to really see Jardine for the first time. He realized it was dawn. Jardine was slumped forward, his left arm cramped around the saddle horn, fingers anchored to his belt. His right hand was pressed high on his shoulder, trying to stop the wound. He'd been hit just under the collarbone. The bullet had gone through, been turned by his shoulder blade, and traveled down. Pecos could feel the hard lump of it just beneath the skin.

Jardine whispered: "What you . . . think . . . Kid?"

"It missed the lung. Get you plugged up, you'll be all right. You can't ride much farther, though. We got to stop pretty soon."

"They're coming, Kid."

"Then we'll fight 'em off."

"To hell . . . with that. Leave me here. No use . . . both of us . . . getting it."

He couldn't leave him there, in the timber. For now, the fire seemed to have made its run below, missing the cañon side, but a shift of wind would bring it back and trap them.

The mountainside seemed gray and endless. At last he found a steep gulch and followed it until he found moss that felt cool through the sides of his boots. Timber grew in isolated clumps, but barring the chance of high wind no fire would spread to them. It was the best he could hope for.

He carried Jardine down, found a hiding place among fallen trunks, fixed him a bed, bandaged him, washed his face with damp moss.

"How you feel?" he asked.

Jardine managed to smile. "I feel good. I just want to lie here. I just want to sleep."

"I'll come back. Listen to me . . . I don't know how long it'll be, but I'll be back."

# XIII

# "AMBUSHED"

He swapped saddles, turned the other horse free. He stood, elbows on the saddle, letting fatigue run out of his body. Above and below lay the vast mountainside. Blending with the gray curtain, it seemed endless. The smoke was dense. He could see less than fifty yards in any direction. Then an eddy brought a long vista into view.

Far downhill, trees rose beyond a rock slide, a knob of stone beyond the trees, and he had an impression of more trees beyond. A bullet stirred rocks with a hard rattle near his feet, the sound of explosion closely after it. Instinctively he went down. His horse, lunging with head up, almost broke away. Holding tight, with the bridle twisted around his left wrist, he let the horse drag him. On one knee, he reached and whipped the carbine from its saddle scabbard.

He didn't fire. Drifting smoke closed in. A second bullet buzzed the air past his cheek. The report was from farther off, from farther to the east. They'd seen him. They were converging on him.

Jardine called, and he answered: "I'm all right. Now keep quiet. I'm leaving, and I'll take them with me."

Mounting the horse, they climbed slowly. After sixty or seventy yards Pecos stopped, waited for the smoke to clear a little. A bullet, singing close, told him he'd been seen. He kept going, taking them at a wide angle away from the wounded man, and stopped at the ridge summit. A cliff dropped off ahead of him. He followed along its rim for about two hundred yards, and reached a spot where it had been cut by a landslide. It was a seventy-degree slope, but he had no choice. They were closing in from two directions.

He dismounted and started down. The horse tried to balk, but Pecos's heavy hand on the bridle brought him along. They slid through rock and dirt and came to a stop above a talus slope.

The talus rock, huge and angular, was almost impassable. What seemed to be a deer trail doubled back along the mountain. He mounted and followed it. It ran along the base of the cliff with a field of giant boulders below. The horse couldn't turn back, so Pecos let the reins hang over the saddle horn and, with his rifle out, kept watch of the cliff rim high overhead.

A horseman appeared, was silhouetted against the smoke-gray sky. He saw Pecos and brought his rifle around to fire, but Pecos took a snap shot with the gunstock cradled in the bend of his arm. The bullet flew a trifle to the right, missed the rider, but scorched the horse. The horse reared. On sloping rock, his legs went from under him. The rider fired wildly. He dropped his rifle and made a grab for leather. The horse dumped him, lunged to his feet, trampled over him, trampled out of sight. The man slipped across the edge of the precipice. He screamed from terror, and for the first time Pecos realized it was Kiowa Johnny.

Kiowa Johnny hung for a second, caught by a rock projection. Then he fell with a shower of stones chasing him. He struck on his back with his arms wide. His broken body was wedged between rocks only an arm's reach from the trail. The broncho, frightened, refused to pass, and Pecos had to dismount, make a blindfold, and lead him.

There were more men above, but Pecos was now hidden

by the slightly overhanging face of the cliff. The trail narrowed. Now it was cliff above and below. He walked with one hand against the rock wall, the other holding the bridle. There was scarcely room for one foot ahead of the other. He didn't look below. He set his mind not to think where one misstep would plummet him.

There was another landslide channel. It placed him briefly into view, and a bullet from long range stirred a geyser of dirt twenty feet below him. He didn't bother to look around. He kept going, on and on, a twisting, slow descent.

He mounted again, rode through wind-twisted dwarf pine. Below, through smoke, he could see the valley bottom with here and there the metallic shine of a stream. He traveled for many minutes. There was no more gunfire, no sign of pursuit. Nearing the base of the steep slope, he saw horsemen below at his right. They'd found a shorter route. They were closing in.

He had little time for decision. He turned sharply and, spurring his horse, tried to escape by a trail through timber. From above, he'd been unable to appraise the rough topography. Now he saw that his course was suicidal. It would take him to a steep switchback, and the switchback would lead him to the bottom directly into their guns.

He slowed his horse. Below, he had seen the roof of a shanty. Closer, near the foot of the slope, lay a rusty heap of dirt. That was a prospecting dump, and its size told him that a tunnel of considerable depth must have been driven into the mountainside. It occurred to him that there'd be an air shaft somewhere close. He reined in. Finally saw it. The air shaft was unmarked by a dump. It had been driven from below in the nature of a raise. Only a cribwork of logs around the collar showed it was there.

He quickly dismounted, looked into its black depths. A

steady upcast of air told him it communicated with the tunnel. No ladder, but pole cribbing and X-pieces had been set to hold the walls. He'd be able to scale it from below without any trouble. Working swiftly, he dragged deadwood branches to conceal the opening. Then, running back to his horse, he mounted and rode down the switchback to the valley bottom.

A rifle bullet whipped past with a sting of closeness. He saw men and fired back rapidly as he could lever his Winchester. His bullets drove them to cover. They were beyond the cabin, among rocks. Content to keep him cornered until help arrived.

Pecos found cover close against the hillside. The mine dump, a flat projection terminating in a pole tipple, gave more concealment. The horse balked at the dark entrance. He blindfolded him, led him inside.

There, in the cool dampness, he sat down with his rifle across his knees, knowing he'd be able to fight back ten men or a hundred.

# XIV

# "THE DEATH SLIDE"

He was tired. His legs felt paralyzed. He dozed between waking and sleeping, and a sound brought him up, alert. Someone had spoken. For an instant he imagined the voice came from the mine depths behind him. Then he realized it was only an echo.

"Pecos!" the voice repeated. It was Mixler.

He didn't answer. He rolled a cigarette, and dry-smoked it.

A stone rattled near the portal. Then Mixler again, closer now. "Pecos! Pecos, can you hear me?"

He didn't answer. The voice kept ringing for a long time in the dark rock walls of the tunnel. It reminded him of Hernandez's guitar, and how, lying close to it in the still, prairie night, one could hear the tiny, ringing sound that always hung to the strings. The mine was like that, if one listened closely enough.

A gunshot deafened him. He had to stand to restrain the horse. Someone had fired upward, into the portal. A sulphurous smell drifted toward him.

"Pecos!" Mixler shouted. "You want to get out of there alive! Then come out with your hands up!"

Alive! His lips twisted in a smile. They'd kill him the second he showed himself in the portal.

"Pecos, we know you're in there. Come out with your hands up!"

He didn't answer. His voice, echoing in the depths, might

have been heard by someone at the air shaft above. He waited and, after a long time, heard a thud and smelled drifting dust as they rolled boulders from above, closing the portal.

It was quite dark. The horse, after some momentary nervousness, stood quietly. Pecos tied him to a timber and groped his way down the tunnel. It was not a crosscut tunnel, driven straight to intercept a vein. It followed the vein and was unpredictably zigzag. Finally he saw light, very dim, from above. The air shaft.

The shaft was also crooked, driven for the twin purposes of ventilation and exploration. He left his rifle and climbed from one timber to the next. It was a couple hundred feet to the top. At last he saw the sky, broken into little, irregular patches by the brush he'd thrown over the shaft collar.

Twenty feet from the surface, he stopped, braced his legs, breathed, listened. There was no sound. He tried to guess at the time. At least half an hour had passed since the portal was closed.

It was not difficult to work his way to the surface through dead branches. Sunlight, coming through smoke and spruce trees, seemed very bright. He paused, listened, and, reassured by the perfect silence, he drew himself over the crib logs, and stood up.

Mixler and his men were gone. He found a wooden bar, levered rock from the tunnel mouth, and rescued his horse. He returned to Jardine, whom he found somewhat stronger, and got him back to the forks of the Ironrod.

All was quiet where the ambush had met them with flame and bullets the night before. The fire had run in long, black fingers across the ridge to the south. He moved among scattered cattle, downstream, and came across Jim Swing, Hernandez, and Wolf Carson around a tiny campfire, siwashing trout on willow sticks.

He asked about Geppert and Pancake. No one had seen them since the night before. He ate, rested an hour, then he got up and swapped saddles on one of the fresh horses.

Hernandez was watching his face. He knew Pecos perhaps better than any man alive, and the expression he read there made him stand, and hitch his gun belt. "You go for a ride, Keed?"

Pecos jerked his head in a nod.

"You maybe have an idea of visiting Mixler?"

"I think it's about time."

Hernandez laughed with a flash of his white teeth. "Now *thees* is the way Pecos should talk. *Thees* is the Pecos I like to ride weeth."

Jim was listening. He stalked forward. "He'll be waitin' for you, Pecos."

"I doubt it. Mixler thinks he's through with me for good. I'll have him pretty much by surprise."

Jim cursed and said: "Well, that means I'll have to ride along and take care of both of you."

They left Wolf Carson to care for Jardine, and rode at a stiff pace downcañon. It was late afternoon, and already growing cool.

"Theenk they went back to the beeg herd?" Hernandez asked.

"I doubt it. They been a night without sleep like us. They'll camp some place. Gets dark, maybe we can spot their fire."

At twilight, they crossed a saddle in the ridge and looked across rolling hill country toward a valley running northwestward toward the Belle Fourche.

"That's Kettle Creek," Pecos said. "I reckon that's where they plugged me in the mine, only yonder, seven or eight miles farther up." He pointed out a place among the hills. "Kettle's pretty dry-bone this time of year, but you can always find good water at Trapper Springs. If I was Mixler, I guess that's where I'd stop."

Through twilight, a glimmer of fire came into view, and Hernandez, with an admiring chuckle, said: "Keed, you have the fine hunch. Why weeth these good hunch are you always the big sucker for roulette?"

Of the three, only Big Jim seemed cautious. They rode around grassy, pine-spotted hillsides, the Pecos Kid slouched in the saddle, hat over his eyes, apparently half asleep. Hernandez was singing softly, in a scarcely audible voice, the words of some border song.

"Damn it, keep still," Jim finally whispered.

Hernandez laughed. His laugh was like quiet music. "Jeem, it make you nervous, the thought that soon I will outdraw *Señor* Shoots-in-the-Back Glynn, so that the twelfth notch in his gun will be for *himself,* and another man will have to carve it for heem!"

"There'll be a hell of a lot of guns besides his."

"So perhaps you would like to make a wager. One thousand dollars, *señor,* that at the payoff it will be Hernandez on his feet and Star Glynn on the ground when. . . ."

"Who'll pay me if you lose?"

"What talk is thees? You perhaps want your Hernandez to live only so you will be able to collect a bet? What kind of a friend are you that you worry about collecting money when the friend of your heart lies dead on the ground?"

"Oh, hell!" said Big Jim.

It had been thirty minutes since they'd seen the fire. Now, in the deepening gulch bottom, it was quite dark. The odor of burning wood came to them on the breeze, and somewhere in the chokeberry bramble a horse snorted.

Pecos said: "This is it!"

"You figure to ride right up?" Big Jim asked.

"No." The Kid pulled in. "Well, maybe I will, at that. Yes, I'll ride up. You boys get on each side." He jerked his head, indicating opposite sides of the gulch. "Stay back a little. Might be a sentry out. I doubt it. Mixler will feel pretty safe, but there might be. If there is, he'll stop me, and I'll let him know you're there. That'll get us through."

He rode alone the last two hundred yards with the firelight broken into irregular patterns by intervening brush. Men were sitting around it. He couldn't tell how many. Someone stood, was bent over, silhouetted, moved away. It might have been Billy Six-Spot.

The path he followed, skirting the brush, was practically free of stones. His horse advanced almost soundlessly. He'd lost track of Hernandez and Jim. No sentry stepped out to meet him. Horses, hobbled and grazing in the bottoms, had their heads up, but his approach didn't make them run.

He pulled in, sat in thoughtful contemplation of the fire for a long thirty seconds. Without looking, he knew that Hernandez had come around on the other side of the brush and dismounted. He heard the slight *clink* of a spur as Hernandez's heel came in contact with the ground.

Pecos dismounted then, tied his horse, and walked through brush, following a narrow little trail, holding twigs away. He stopped at the edge of firelight. Men were sitting and lying on the ground. Across the fire, staring at him, lay Andy Rasmussen.

Andy had seen him. His eyes were fixed, staring. His jaw had sagged. He didn't seem to be breathing. He'd been eating a broiled, whole grouse, and in amazement he'd lowered it until it lay in the dirt.

Pecos grinned at him. It wasn't a pleasant grin. He disliked Rasmussen, had contempt for him, and the smile showed it.

There were six men by the fire. Besides Rasmussen, there were Star Glynn, Billy Six-Spot, Ellis Haltman, a cowboy called Alky, and Mixler. He wondered about Evas Williams. Maybe Evas had been killed.

Mixler was sitting cross-legged, his back turned. The long trail from Texas had taken him down, removed the last ounce of fat from him, dehydrated him, and yet he was big. Big like a bull elk just through a hard winter.

Mixler was talking. Something about the herd. ". . . no, when that fire runs out, they'll drift back with the grass and water. We'll hold the main bunch on the Belle Fourche and send back for 'em. A few days' graze won't hurt. We'll be across the Yellowstone long before September first."

Billy Six-Spot, noticing the fixed nature of Rasmussen's gaze, turned and saw the Pecos Kid. He started, as though to lunge to his feet, and paused on one knee. It was almost reflex to reach for his gun, but he checked himself.

"Sure, Billy, live for a while," said Pecos, and stepped into the firelight.

Men sprang to their feet, but nobody went for his gun. Mixler was up. Huge and erect, he took a backward step. For just a second his face was slack with surprise, as though he was staring at a ghost.

Pecos said: "Funny thing about miners . . . they generally dig two holes, just like a prairie dog."

Mixler recovered himself. He showed his powerful teeth in something that resembled a smile. "Well, I'll be damned! You know, Pecos, a man's got to admire your kind of guts. I'm going to kill you, but I still got to admire your kind of guts."

"Takes guts to come here alone, all right. Of course, there's a chance I'm not alone. That's something you have to gamble on." As he talked, his eyes were on Mixler, but he

230

kept watch on the others, too, and, when Glynn, looking very slack and casual, started to drop back, he said: "Now, Star, that might be a number-one way of committing suicide. How you know but what I got six men out in the bushes? Why, six men would take care of everyone here."

Rasmussen said in a whisper, scarcely audible: "He was alone up the cañon. He was holed up alone. Rest of 'em scattered. He's bluffing."

Still watching Mixler, Pecos spoke to Rasmussen: "If you believe that, try going for your gun."

Rasmussen wouldn't do it. Mixler, perhaps, or Glynn, or Six-Spot, but not Rasmussen.

Pecos said: "I came for you, Mixler. Before heading over the ridge for Deadwood, I came for you."

Mixler's eyes kept moving around, probing the shadows. He licked his lips. He jerked his shoulders back with a brittle laugh. "But you got an ace in the hole."

"Nobody's going to kill you but me. I got a proposition for you. You leave your men by the fire. We'll walk over there, across the creek. There's not much light, but there's enough. We'll settle it there, the two of us. But maybe you haven't got that kind of guts."

Mixler's lips twisted down. He hated Pecos. He'd hated him from the first night when he'd noticed the girl, Lita Haltman, watching him.

"Why, you cheap gunhawk," Mixler spat. He stood with his hands on his hips. "I'll fight you with guns, or I'll fight you with my hands. And when I'm through, you won't go over the ridge to Deadwood. You won't go anywhere. To hell with crossing the creek, Pecos, you're just ten yards away from being a dead man."

Mixler stood with massive shoulders sloped forward a trifle. His eyes were very intent on Pecos. Beyond him, Star

Glynn was on one knee, staring beyond them into the dark.

Neither Hernandez nor Big Jim was in that direction. The warning hit Pecos like the buzz of a rattler. It was Evas Williams. He'd been standing guard somewhere. Now he was coming up from the shadow.

Pecos turned casually, and dove to one side. Guns exploded at the same instant. Two guns, one so close on the other their reports mingled. A bullet had slugged him in the left shoulder. It was like being struck by a hammer. The scene seemed to veer, to slide across his eyeballs. He saw Mixler draw. Flame and explosion burst in his face. He could feel the whip and burn of powder.

It all happened in an instant, while he was on his way to the ground. His own gun was in his hand. He had no memory of drawing it. It was merely there. It seemed to aim and fire by itself. He was dully conscious of the hard buck of it at the same instant his outflung left hand touched the earth.

Mixler was hit. He reeled, clutching his throat with his left hand, six-shooter still in his right. The Kid hit him with a second slug. Mixler still had his gun. It kept pouring flame and lead. He was firing blindly into the ground. A third bullet sent him reeling back. Still he didn't go down. He half turned. Now his back was toward Pecos. He fired the last shot from the magazine. It tore a furrow through the fire. He took four or five gargantuan, stumbling steps. Star Glynn lay dead, face down, and Mixler trod over him. Then he fell. His head was almost in the fire. He tried to get up. He reached and clawed a handful of coals. Then the life left his muscles, and he slid on his forehead across the ground.

There was shooting in the outer darkness. The Kid kept trying to gather his thoughts. At last he heard Hernandez's voice.

"You all right, Keed?"

Pecos looked up. Hernandez was crouched in the opening between two chokeberry bushes, punching spent cartridges from his gun.

"I don't know. I feel like somebody hit me with a hammer. I feel like I just woke up from a three-day drunk."

"Ha! You are now dreaming of Deadwood. Tonight you took a bullet in the left arm. Look, your shirt sleeve is all heavy weeth blood. It was that bushwhacker, Evas Williams. I saw the shine of his gun just as he fired, so, alas, I had not the time to save you from your wound."

"What the hell happened? That's Star Glynn, isn't it?"

"Sure, did I not say it would be thus? Did I not say I would pay heem for the bushwhack of Reavley? Also, I have won back one thousand dollars from that miser, Jim Swing. Fccfty more nights like this will see your Hernandez freed of his awful burden of debt. Now sit still, and I will bandage the wound."

"I'm all right. Where's Jim?" He called: "Jim!"

Jim's voice came from the uphill shadow. "Here! But you better stomp that fire out or they'll circle and make wolf meat of you."

Hernandez laughed with a bright flash of his teeth. He had his shirt off, tearing it in strips for bandage. "No. They will have little fight left. What was it the poet said? . . . *when the head is chopped off, the bird theenk only of flapping his wings.* So with these gunmen, I theenk they will fly far and stop only to fight when another man has dollars to pay them."

Geppert and Pancake had returned to the camp on Ironrod, when they got back. Two days were spent hunting cattle, and with most of the herd they pushed over a high backbone of the country toward Spearfish.

It was evening, and Pecos, riding the drag, reined in to roll himself a leisurely cigarette. He looked back and to the north. There were foothills, prairie, the purplish breaks of the Belle Fourche, and more prairie. Still farther, over the uncertain, grayish horizon, lay the Yellowstone, and after the Yellowstone, the vast, almost untouched plains of Montana, the land where grass grew to a tall steer's belly.

Hernandez saw him and came back at a gallop. "Keed! Why do you stop? We must hurry. Just over the hill, maybe two, three days away, is there not the lights and women? Is there not music and good red wine? Is there not the Deadwood of our dreams?" He closed his eyes, entranced, and strummed a dream guitar, singing lazily.

*¡Ay, ay, ay, ay!*
*¡Canta no llores¡*

"Sure, Butch. I'm sure with you for that Deadwood."

He was thinking that he'd have to spend a week in Deadwood. Hernandez would be broke by that time. Broke and borrowing money. In three weeks he'd have all of them broke. He'd leave after a week, while they still had something left. With fresh horses, they could head back up the Belle Fourche, cross the Little Missouri, and meet the herd somewhere close to the Yellowstone.

It would be tough on the Haltmans, taking that big herd through. He had nothing against the Haltmans. Ellis was a hothead, but lots of men are hotheads at the age of twenty-one. Vern and Tommy were all right. And Lita. . . .

Sometimes, at the most unexpected moment, the memory of Lita would hit him, and she'd be there again, beside him, slim and eager, her hand on his shirt, her dark eyes looking up at him. Yes, Lita was all right, too.

# ABOUT THE AUTHOR

Dan Cushman was born in Osceola, Michigan, and grew up on the Cree Indian Reservation in Montana. He graduated from the University of Montana with a Bachelor of Science degree in 1934 and pursued a career in mining as a prospector, assayer, and geologist before turning to journalism. In the early 1940s his novelette-length stories began appearing regularly in such Fiction House magazines as *North-West Romances* and *Frontier Stories*. Later in the decade his North-Western and Western stories as well as fiction set in the Far East and Africa began appearing in *Action Stories*, *Adventure*, and *Short Stories*. A collection of some of his best North-Western and Western fiction has recently been published, VOYAGEURS OF THE MIDNIGHT SUN (1995), with a Foreword by John Jakes who cites Cushman as a major influence in his own work. The character, Comanche John, a Montana road agent featured in numerous rollicking magazine adventures, also appears in Cushman's first novel, MONTANA, HERE I BE (1950) and in two later novels. STAY AWAY, JOE, which first appeared in 1953, is an amusing novel about the mixture, and occasional collision, of Indian culture and Anglo-American culture among the Métis (French Indians) living on a reservation in Montana. The novel became a bestseller and remains a classic to this day, greatly loved especially by Indian peoples for its truthfulness and humor. Yet, while humor became Cushman's hallmark in such later novels as THE OLD COPPER COLLAR (1957) and

GOOD BYE, OLD DRY (1959), he also produced significant historical fiction in THE SILVER MOUNTAIN (1957), concerned with the mining and politics of silver in Montana in the 1890s. This novel won a Spur Award from the Western Writers of America. His fiction remains notable for its breadth, ranging all the way from a story of the cattle frontier in TALL WYOMING (1957) to a poignant and memorable portrait of small-town life in Michigan just before the Great War in THE GRAND AND THE GLORIOUS (1963). THE PECOS KID RETURNS will be his next **Five Star Western**.